Mark's Remarkable

Summer

By

Jan Moon

This is a work of fiction. All characters, with the one exception of the ref-erences to Josh McDowell, are strictly products of the author's imagina-tion.

ISBN-13: 978-0615888774

ISBN-10: 0615888771

Mark's Remarkable

Summer

All scripture references are taken from the King James version of the Bible.

Dedicated with all my love to the memory of my wonderful husband, Cecil L. Moon Jr., who stood by me through so much. To say he was wonderful is such a vast understatement as to be almost unlawful. He was my life; he loved the Lord, and he constantly inspired me in all my endeavors.

Chapter One

1988

Busted again. He'd almost made it to the front gate when his mother's voice stopped him in his tracks. "Mark, have you forgotten you were going to mow the Barbours' grass?"

Of course he hadn't forgotten. It was just that he really, really needed to get downtown before they rented out *Beverly Hills Cop II*. Hemlock, Missouri, was a small town, and the guys at the video store never got more than one or two copies of anything, no matter how good it was. And he knew this was super good, because he'd heard it had grossed more than $150,000,000. That was a lot of money. And he'd missed it because he was grounded the week it played in Grover last year.

Mark hated to whine, but he sure didn't want to do the Barbours' lawn today. In fact, he'd planned on doing it tomorrow morning because he and Herb and Carl had big plans for tonight. It was the official last day of the lull between school letting out for the summer and summer school starting. They were planning on going to Carl's and hanging out at the boathouse. They'd watch the movie and by that time Carl's parents would be in bed. Then they'd raid the fridge and take everything down to the lake. Herb had bestowed one of his stupid, lopsided winks upon them when he'd told them he'd bring "something special," meaning his brother Kyle was home from college for the summer and had probably brought a stash of weed. Actually, sometimes Mark didn't think it was so great. It stunk, it gave him a headache, but it didn't really give him any kind of a buzz. Maybe there was something wrong with it. Or with him. However, he always joined in just to be sociable or, more likely, because he didn't want to look like a dork in front of his best friends. Now, he half-turned and scuffed his Nikes on the walk. "I'm doing it tomorrow. Me and the guys are gonna get together later and I promised I'd pick up the movie."

His mother grimaced and shifted Mark's little sister to her other hip. "The guys and I," she corrected.

"Whatever," Mark mumbled.

The baby waved one arm and chanted, "Ga ga ga."

Brat.

Mom relented a little. "All right, get the movie, but come right back and do the lawn. You'll have time before you meet the boys. Tomorrow is Sunday and you know Hilda has church at the cabin. You can't be running the mower during church."

Aw, geez, he'd thought today was Friday and tomorrow was Saturday. Mark muttered something he was glad his mom couldn't hear and then said, "Okay. I'll be back in a while."

"Thank you, son," his mother called.

Maureen Stone watched her only son walk out of the gate and get into his 1972 Chevy Nova, a gift from his father on his seventeenth birthday last November. Actually, the present was from both of them, but it had been Richard's idea. Maureen couldn't bring herself to face the reality of her firstborn being old

7

enough to drive, let alone his own car. Never mind that he was six feet tall and looked like a Greek god with two left feet, or that on the football field he was a killer.

The car wasn't much to look at, but the engine was sound, and that was more important than beauty. Mark and Richard had gone to a junk yard and found a door to replace the passenger door, which had been dented so badly it wouldn't close. The new door was maroon, but at least it closed, and Mark didn't seem to mind the maroon door in the blue car. He'd probably spend all his spare time for the next few years working on that car. Maybe it was worth it, if it would keep him out of trouble.

***

Mark drove slowly down the hill. Actually, he could have walked to the video store. But he loved the feel of his own car. He'd had it for nearly eight months, but he still got a thrill when he turned his own key in his own ignition and heard the engine roar to life. His very own engine. It was so cool.

He started mumbling to himself as he thought about having to mow that grass today. He actually didn't mind mowing the grass, had been doing it for years, but why did Hilda Barbour have to have church at her house? It wasn't natural. Church should be held in buildings with pews and steeples, the way God intended. Hilda's church had been destroyed in a fire last year. They were re-building just outside of town but the funding was slow in coming and it would probably be late fall before it was completed. After the members got their act to-gether following the fire, they gravitated to Hilda's house for their services during the winter. When the Hilda and Malcolm moved to the lake, a bunch of men got together and thinned out a dozen oak trees from the woods adjacent to the cabin. They arranged them in rows facing the lake and put up a crude wooden cross and a pulpit. They met there every Sunday morning and evening and Wednesday night in good weather. When it rained, they crowded into the cabin. Hilda's husband, Malcolm, didn't even go to Hilda's Sunday service, for Pete's sake. He was Catholic and always went to Saturday mass so that Sunday mornings he could go and hang out with his friends at the Coffee Café, the gathering place for every man in town between the ages of 18 and 98.

Mark and his family attended a non-denominational church downtown, but didn't go very often, just Christmas and Easter and a few times during the year. They always meant to go but never could get themselves together. Mark's father owned the funeral home and he was always busy. Even though he had help, and even though Hemlock was a small town, Stone and Griswold Funeral Home was the only mortuary in this end of the county. In addition to the regular funerals, the coroner kept them busy, too. But at least when they went to church it was in a real church and not rows of logs by the lake. Of course it wasn't the fault of the members of Hilda's church that it had burned to the ground last year.

The agonizing irony was that Deborah Stringer's father was pastor of Hilda's church. Mark had had a crush on Deborah Stringer since she moved to town with her parents three years ago. After their arrival the church had started growing, and Mark had suggested to his parents once or twice that they try attending. They just looked at him and asked, "Why?" and that settled that. He could have gone alone, but he was afraid it would be too obvious. On the football field he was in his element, but when it came to dating he was a disaster. Then

9

the church burned down and he abandoned the idea. Now lately, Mom had started attending Mrs. Stringer's Bible study. Just what the significance of that was Mark couldn't begin to fathom., but he intended to keep a close eye on developments.

Mark was in luck. The video store had *Beverly Hills Cop II*. He rented it, got back in his car and allowed himself a brief 90 mph ride on the four-lane. Plenty of time to get the grass mowed and get to Carl's. Life was good.

***

"Mark, come in and have some pie before you leave," Hilda called from the kitchen window as Mark passed by on his way to the shed to put the mower away.

"Yes, ma'am," Mark replied, resisting the urge to glance at his watch. He had time. It wasn't as if he was on a timetable; he'd get there when he got there. He grinned to himself. He'd tell the guys Hilda gave him a piece of her pie and they'd be jealous. Hilda's pies were known far and wide. She baked nearly every weekend for some bake sale somewhere, even bake sales other churches held. She always baked an extra one just for sampling.

Mark put the mower away and then washed his hands at the outside spigot. Drying them on his jeans, he entered the cabin to the sound of Hilda's humming coming from the kitchen. Hilda was always humming old show tunes. The reason Mark knew this was because he'd heard Malcolm tell someone once that Hilda knew every song from every Broadway show before 1970.

Mark had always thought the Barbour cabin was pretty cool. The living room-dining area occupied the front. In the back were two tiny bedrooms, with a bathroom between them. A kitchen had been added onto the dining area, sticking out like an appendage from the rest of the cabin. All the spare wall space was occupied with bookcases overflowing with books, and Mark was constantly overwhelmed at the number of volumes. Over the years, Hilda and Malcolm had loaned him and many other kids anything they had needed or wanted for school. Until a couple of years ago Hemlock hadn't had a library. Except for the small school library and the weekly traveling library out of Grover, the Barbours had been the only source of books available for borrowing for kids and adults alike.

Mark stood in front of the bookcase that held the entire Encyclopedia Britannica, about a gazillion other reference books, two whole shelves of Bibles in varying states of wear, and very little else. On the wall over the bookcase was a framed picture of what he supposed to be Jesus knocking on a door that had no handle. It looked very old, or at least the frame did. Mark wondered if the artist had left the handle off the door on purpose or if it was an oversight. He'd have to ask Hilda. Sometime.

"Hello, Mark. I see you've discovered my birthday present." Hilda bustled in from the kitchen, bearing a tall glass of milk and a piece of apple pie the size of catcher's mitt.

"Um, yes, ma'am."

Wonderful. Was that the only thing he could come up with to say to Hilda?

Hilda didn't seem to notice. She set the plate and glass on the table and pulled a napkin from the pocket of her denim skirt. "Sit down and cool off. Goodness, what a hot summer already! How are your mother and dad?" Hilda sat

11

down opposite Mark.

"They're fine. Busy. Mom's on the Hemlock Centennial committee," Mark managed around a mouthful of pie. His eyes drifted to the picture and he tore them away, still wondering about the door handle.

"Revelation 3:20. *Christ at Heart's Door.* 'Behold I stand at the door and knock; if anyone hears my voice and opens the door, I will come in to him and will dine with him and he with me.' My sister sent it from Independence. The print is rather dog-eared but the frame is antique. Mal cleaned it up and put new glass in it. Isn't it beautiful?" Hilda looked up at the picture, her face wreathed in a smile.

In Mark's opinion the picture was old, faded, and barely okay. But beautiful it was not.

Hilda cocked her head to one side. "I think we'll start with the Book of John. Right now I know you have plans," Hilda said as she stood and picked up Mark's plate and empty glass. "Have a good time and don't let anyone talk you into anything." She reached into the pocket of her skirt and brought out a ten dollar bill. "Thanks again for everything you do for us." She went on. "Do you have a Bible?"

Mark took the money and said, "Thank *you.* Um, yes. Well, no. I mean, I have one of those kid ones. You know, with pictures of stuff."

He wanted to slap himself upside the head. How totally dumb could he sound?

"Wait a minute," said Hilda as she scurried over to the bookcase and selected a smallish, well-worn paperback. She handed it to him and instructed,

12

"Just look it over. Get a feel for it. Read a little bit. That's all. I know you're busy."

Mark looked at the book cover, which read: *New Testament, Psalms and Proverbs.*

He looked at Hilda, who was watching him expectantly.

Uh oh, she's going to try to give me some religion again, thought Mark.

"As I said, you don't have to read it cover to cover just now. But read The Gospel of John, and a couple of the Psalms. And remember, God loves you."

"Uh, okay," Mark managed as he headed toward the door. "Thanks, Hilda."

"You're welcome," called Hilda as Mark jumped into his car.

During the short drive back to town Mark replayed Hilda's last instruction and very presumptuous plans for him. The Gospel of John. He knew it was in the New Testament but that was about all. He didn't even know for sure what the word "gospel" meant. *". . . Don't let anyone talk you into anything."* Huh.

***

Two puffs of dust from Mark's tires didn't settle quite as quickly as the dust that surrounded them. They continued to gyrate by the roadside, unnoticed by anything or anyone. Not quite formed, yet not like quite like their surroundings, they stirred lazily on the dry, lifeless roadway. One spoke. "I think our job just got easier."

Klork wished his companion didn't shout so loudly. A normal tone would do. But there was nothing normal about Muco. He, like Klork, was just another one of Satan's minions, unseen to humans, but determined to continue wreaking havoc among the people wherever they encountered a need for chaos.

"This Stone kid," Muco bellowed, "is starting to come around. I was worried about him for a while. But his stupidity may just keep him in our hands." He shook a bony, invisible finger at Klork and then went back to puffing on his fag.

As minions they were so far down the ladder they weren't even known by Satan, who had millions of agents doing far more important things, such as attending crusades where the leader actually used a Bible and preached the Gospel. These two had never been allowed near a Billy Graham Crusade; they just didn't have the fortitude. Oh, they were pure evil, but it would take several more millennia for them to develop enough polish for events such as that.

Now they'd been sent back to Hemlock, Missouri, to the scene of the crime, as it were, to check on a possible problem. The cosmic rumor mill had it that there was a danger of a revival. Last year they "helped" the faulty wiring in the local Baptist Church and watched with glee as the old wooden building went up like a Fourth of July firecracker. That sent the congregation to the four winds. Some of the intrepid ones, of course, had stuck around to rebuild, but the rest of the flock drifted to other churches and some even started attending that mega church in Independence, where thousands of "worshippers" did everything but declare the Gospel. They didn't need much attention at all; they were already lost. Praise to the Evil One!

Klork spoke, his voice like that of a feral cat, somewhere between a hiss and a purr. "Don't sell that old woman short. She's got that kid in her sights and I wouldn't put anything past her. She just gave him The Book, or didn't you notice?"

Muco waved him away with a cloud of smoke. "Yeah yeah yeah, so he's got The Book. He'll take it home, and if he remembers to take it out of his car he'll put it under a pile of other books and forget about it. That old broad's got no hold on him," he shrieked. "She's just some old lady who hires him to mow her lawn. The kid's more interested in smoking dope and getting that preacher's chick in his car."

"Don't be too sure, Mr. Know It All. I don't like it that his old lady has started going to those Bible classes Mrs. Goodie Two-Shoes is teaching," Klork replied as the puffs of dust dissipated into the late afternoon haze.

***

"Yo, Stone! Get your butt in here," shouted Carl from his front doorway as Mark pulled up to the house. "We're waitin' on that movie. You did bring it, didn't you?"

Carl wasn't bothered by finesse.

The evening passed in a haze of pizza, ice cream, Carl's Mom's brownies and Axel Foley's hysterical antics. Now Carl's parents were in bed and it was time to do some serious damage to the family food supply. They loaded up coolers with bread, cold cuts, chips, soda, the rest of the brownies, and enough condiments for a large family reunion. Plus Carl's boom box and tapes, covering everything from The Doors to the Grateful Dead.

The boathouse had a second story, used for storage, but enjoyed by Carl and his sister for overnights. They had taken turns when they were younger, but now that Kate was away at college, Carl had it all to himself. His parents had set ground rules years ago, that stood firmly now, with addenda as the children got older: no boating after dark; no swimming after dark unless one of the adults was present and all the outside lights were on; noise level at a minimum—if Carl's parents could hear them in the house, it was too noisy; no members of the opposite sex after dark; absolutely no alcohol or drugs, including nicotine.

The kids had stuck to the rules for the most part. Carl couldn't speak for Kate, but figured she and her friends were such goody-goodies it probably wouldn't even occur to them to do anything AGAINST THE RULES. The boys hadn't gotten caught at the rest of the infractions. For some reason swimming, boating and the opposite sex hadn't been much of an issue, and the noise usually leveled out after midnight. But once in a great while one of the kids would smuggle in either beer or marijuana. This was rare and in small quantities, and getting rid of the evidence took some creative thinking.

Now, though, Herb's brother had returned from his second year of college, and who knew what he'd brought back for them to try? As Mark and Herb unrolled sleeping bags and staked out individual spaces, Carl set up the boom box and turned on Led Zeppelin. He turned around and started doing his really obnoxious air guitar thing and then grabbed Herb's knapsack.

"So, Herb, baby, watcha got?"

"Hey hey hey!" Herb grabbed the bag and stuck it in his sleeping bag. "Easy, don't damage the merchandise."

"Yeah, yeah, don't be stingy," Carl persisted.

"Okay." Herb pulled the bag out and opened it. He reached in and came out with a zip-lock plastic sack. He tossed it to Mark. "Here, Mr. Expert Roller, do it."

Mark caught the sack and held it to the light, in this case one of the flashlights they had arranged around the perimeter of their space. The contents of the sack could have passed for that herb stuff his mother used in spaghetti sauce. Oregano, basil, something like that. Nah. He opened the sack and pulled out the cigarette papers.

***

"Man, am I hungry." Herb hit the button on his Indiglo watch and mumbled, "Two-thirty. Yeesh."

Mark rolled over. "Shut up."

Carl slept on.

Herb groped around in one of the coolers and came up with a foil-wrapped package. "I hope these are the brownies. Those brownies are go-od."

"Well, they're not brownies. I ate the last one around midnight. You lose." Mark flipped over onto his stomach, sleeping bag and all. The heavy, sickish sweet smell of pot hung in the air despite the three big, open windows, and his head was beginning to ache.

Don't let anyone talk you into anything.

The foil-wrapped package turned out to be half a sandwich that Mark hadn't wanted.

"Want this?" asked Herb, holding the soggy mess in Mark's face.

"Uh-uh."

Mark drifted off to sleep to the sounds of Herb munching. A little while later he heard the top pop off a soda and the sound of Herb guzzling.

"Herb."

"Huh?"

"Shut up."

"Man, I'm just getting a drink," Herb whined. "Hey, wanna do another joint?"

Mark yawned and flipped back over onto his back. "No."

"Aw, c'mon, man. Carl won't even wake up and we can have it all to ourselves."

Mark's headache was developing into a major discomfort. He opted for reason instead of hardball. "It's two-thirty in the morning, we've lucked out so far, and Carl's father is a *cop*, fer cryin' out loud."

Silence. Then the flashlight flicked off. Herb made a production out of burrowing back down into his sleeping bag among many sighs, snorts and other disgruntled sounds.

"So, when did you get so chicken over this stuff?"

Mark counted to ten. Then he counted to twenty. Deep breath. "Y'know, Herb, maybe being chicken is being sensible."

"Oh, right. Here we are with a bunch of this really cool weed and you two poop out on me," Herb grumbled.

Carl stuck his head up, his unruly blond hair flopping into his eyes. "Hey, dude, we'll do it again tomorrow night. I mean tonight; it's already tomorrow, and speaking of tomorrow, I've gotta work. The Winklers are re-building their pier and my dad volunteered me."

"Yeesh," said Herb, again.

More silence. Then Herb piped up, "You lucky dog. Marcia is home for the summer, and she is hot! Have you seen her?"

18

"Herbert, Marcia Winkler has always been hot. She's *nineteen*." The non-sequitur rolled off Carl's tongue with little apparent effort.

"So? I'm seventeen. Almost," persisted Herb.

"Yeah, right. Like in January. Eight months."

"Hey, guys?" Mark.

"Huh?"

"Shut up."

"Okay, but I'll make you a bet. I'll bet I get a date with Marcia Winkler before the end of June."

Mark snorted and Carl replied, "Get real, dude. Why would she go out with you? You're younger than her little brother. And why would you want to date a nineteen-year-old girl? She's not even a girl. She's an older woman. She's in college, probably dating the football team."

"Okay, that's it. I'm outta here. I'll sleep in my car." Mark slithered out of his sleeping bag and started putting on his shoes.

Herb grabbed his arm. "Wait, wait, wait. Okay, I'll shut up. Just take the bet—uh—ten bucks." He wore that determined look that Mark and Carl had come to know. Wide eyes, half a smile, and an "I'm not going away until you agree" posture that had gotten the three of them in more hot water than they cared to recall.

This time it was Carl who said, "Yeesh." Mark said something else.

"Are you that mad at your money?" Carl asked in all sincerity. But he stuck out his hand and they shook on it. Mark had burrowed back down and was waiting for Herb to make good on his promise to shut up.

"Stone!" Mark ignored him.

"Hey, Stone!"

"What!" Someday he was going to do some serious injury to his pal Herb.

"Shake on it, dude."

Mark stuck out his hand and mumbled several all-purpose words that might have been nouns, verbs, adverbs, adjectives or prepositions; it didn't matter.

"... *talk you in to anything.*"

"End of June," Herb whispered. "G'night."

No answer.

Chapter Two

Hilda Barbour was sixty-nine years old, looked fifty, and felt forty most of the time. In fact, if it weren't for her arthritis, she would still be riding horseback and roller skating. Now she stuck with bowling and walking two miles a day. She just couldn't reconcile being in her sixties when mentally she was still in her twenties. It was an aspect of the aging process on which she didn't quite agree with God. But she planned on asking Him about it when she saw Him. Meanwhile, there was plenty to do right here and now.

She and Malcolm would celebrate their fiftieth wedding anniversary in September. They were childless, and stood at opposite ends of the spectrum as far as religion was concerned. Malcolm was raised Roman Catholic, and had watched with a great deal of interest the changes which had taken place within his church. From Vatican II to an emerging scandal in the Boston area involving every level of the clergy. But he continued to attend mass, went to confession at Christmas and Easter, even got ashes on his forehead on Ash Wednesday most years. He liked the monotony of the mass, the predictability of the rituals. He could remain relatively anonymous and not worry about working too hard at being Catholic.

Hilda had come from fundamental evangelical roots, but had come to a saving knowledge of Jesus only after attending a revival with her cousin while Malcolm was overseas during the war. She had tremblingly walked down the aisle to the front of the tent when the preacher's one word pierced her heart. "Lost." Then she had prayed for forty-eight years for Malcolm to come to the same saving grace. A few times over the years, Malcolm had accompanied her, and had even asked a number of questions concerning the church. In the early days, Hilda

21

would get her hopes up, thinking Malcolm was ready to be converted, but she soon learned that he was just being polite, trying to please her.

Mark was another matter. Hilda had watched him grow up, just as she had watched an entire generation of Hemlock raised and educated. Then they either left or settled down in the tiny town, whose only claim to fame was that it was halfway between Kansas City and Columbia, home of the university.

Maybe it was his disarming smile, one he'd unconsciously cultivated since he was a baby, but wasn't aware of yet. Or his hunger for learning everything about everything, which had gotten him into nearly constant trouble from the time he was a toddler. The most famous incident was when he had received a recorder for his eighth birthday, and he wanted to see if he could be the Pied Piper. He let all the Crowders' goats out in hopes they would follow him. They didn't, and it was several days before they got them all rounded up.

Maybe it was the shock of light red hair that always fell over his left eye the way Hilda's brother's had. Ned had been shot down over Germany in 1943, at age nineteen, the year before she met Malcolm. To this day, every time Mark tossed his hair out of his eyes Hilda would see her baby brother. Ned had shunned religion of any kind. It wasn't that he didn't believe in God. He was just too busy and figured he had time to do something about that—after the war. At that age he probably thought himself immortal, the way so many young people do.

Because Hilda and Malcolm didn't have children of their own, they acted as unofficial surrogate parents to the kids of Hemlock. Now, most of those kids had kids of their own, so now they were surrogate grandparents. Everyone loved

22

the Barbours.

Mark started tending the Barbours' yards when he was twelve and could handle a power mower. Now, after nearly five years, he knew every inch of both yards better than either Hilda or Malcolm, and even took a proprietary interest in their properties. Not a weed escaped his scrutiny, or a mole, or anything else that would interfere with the perfection of the lawns. Hilda handled the flowers, but the lawns were Mark's. He took a great deal of pride in his work. Malcolm was delighted he didn't have to be involved in any of it. He was free to pursue his sometimes-lucrative hobby of collecting old—very old—first edition books.

Hilda was very pleased with the way yesterday had gone. Mark hadn't scoffed at or discounted what she had told him about Revelation and the picture. Of course, she had barely scratched the surface, but he seemed surprisingly receptive. Hilda had prayed earnestly for this opportunity, never dreaming that it would come through a simple picture. But she'd seen Mark's apparent interest. Maybe it had been just curiosity. But still, it was something. She was surprised that Mark hadn't recognized the verse, but then, who knew what went on at that feel-good church he and his family sometimes attended?

She had been praying for Mark for several years but recently had seen some changes in him that concerned her. He sometimes seemed aloof, or distracted. Of course, he'd been the recipient of testosterone overload for the last few years, just as any other red-blooded boy falls victim to. He was also way involved in football, which was perfectly normal at his age. But there was something else. A hardening, a coldness that she hadn't been aware of before. She needed to rev up her praying; she didn't like what she was suspecting.

***

"Mark, I need you to help me do some rearranging," said Richard as Mark came in from Carl's house.

Oh, no. They'd gotten a delivery of two caskets Friday and they had to be put on display. They weighed a ton and they gave Mark the creeps. Even though he'd been brought up in the business, he just couldn't work up any enthusiasm for how his dad made his living. The funeral home had most of its caskets displayed just as fractional-cuts mounted into permanent modules on the walls. But Dad always kept at least two complete units as well. They were on carts with casters, but they still had to be maneuvered into positions in the display room, and that never worked out well. Space was cramped, and Mark always felt as if he was wrestling a 2000-pound robot.

"Okay, Dad." Why couldn't Dad have been a lawyer, like Herb's Dad? Or a cop, like Carl's? Nope, had to be an undertaker. A mortician. A funeral director. No matter what you called it, it still dealt with dead people. Mom had told him time and time again that it was a calling, and that it was an integral part of the life cycle. Yeah, right. Big ceremony and show-off time for Aunt Bessie. "Doesn't she look like herself?" No, she looks dead.

Mark skipped the shower, knowing he'd just get sweaty again, so he brushed his teeth, swiped at his face with a wet washcloth, and ran his fingers through his hair. Then he followed his Dad next door to the funeral home. The two houses were actually connected by a tunnel, a byproduct of the Underground Railroad during Civil War, but in the summer it was just as easy to cross the driveway.

24

"So, did you guys have a good time last night?" Richard asked as they wheeled in the first casket, a steel monstrosity that had to weigh twelve thousand pounds.

"Uh, it was okay." Did Dad suspect anything? Why was he asking him about last night?

"Nice of Carl's folks to let you do that all the time."

Do what? What was he talking about? Did he mean the pot? Why was he being so cool about it? Mark started to sweat. He knew he should answer, but he didn't know what to say. He swallowed once. Then he swallowed again. His mouth was so dry he nearly choked.

"They've been letting you all use that boathouse for quite a while. Your mom and I have been talking with the Turners, thinking we ought to reciprocate in some way. I mean other than the barbeques and things. How would you feel about a trip to Yellowstone, maybe at the end of August?"

Mark's breath rushed out in a gasp and he realized he'd been holding it so long he was dizzy. Dad wasn't talking about the pot. He was referring to a genuine way of saying thank you to the Hillmans for their hospitality.

"Uh, yeah, that'd be great." Mark had to clear his throat.

Did his voice sound as weird to his father as it did to him? Apparently not, because Dad continued, "It might take a bit of coordination, getting vacations lined up, but I'm pretty sure Pete Norris can cover for me for a week while I'm gone."

Pete Norris was another undertaker, from Columbia, a friend of Dad's, the two of them having covered time off for each other over the years.

"Herb's dad can take off any time now that he has that paralegal working for him. And Phil has vacation time coming; shouldn't be any problem," Dad finished as they positioned the casket under the painting of a white dove that looked like it was flying out of an exploding bank vault. Mark knew it was supposed to be Heaven, but it just didn't quite get it. The light beams looked more like gold coins, and the clouds were too dark, like molten steel.

"Great," repeated Mark, suddenly so overcome with guilt he couldn't think of one more word to say to his father.

Richard took out his handkerchief and swiped at an area on the lid of the casket. "Well, we'll work on it. Don't say anything to the other two just yet, because we'll be going anyway. I just wanted to give you a heads up, let you know what we had up our sleeves."

"Yeah, thanks, Dad," Mark said as he started toward the back portico where the other casket waited to be moved into its new temporary home.

"Mark, Carl called," said Mom when they came back in. "Were you planning on staying over there again tonight? I need you to baby sit. Dad and I are going to a movie."

"That's okay. Go ahead and I'll stay home. I've got to start reading for *Shakespeare*." The guilt was still eating him alive. Tomorrow it would be gone and he'd be back on track, but for now, he needed to play it cool.

"You don't get any sleep there, anyway," Mom went on.

If she only knew.

"We don't mind you doing it once or twice a week if it's all right with the Turners, but more than that is too much. Besides, Dad needs you here to help

26

him now that Mr. Griswold is retiring."

Mark sighed. "Mr. Griswold is never going to retire. He's been talking about it since I was Rachael's age. He'll still be talking about it when Dad retires."

"No, I really think he's going to this time," said Dad, taking the pitcher of iced tea from the refrigerator.

Mom took out three glasses and began filling them with ice. "He's not well. These last couple of years, since Bernice died, I guess, it's almost as if he's been . . . I don't know . . . waiting for his turn."

"Ma, that's morbid," protested Mark.

Dad poured the tea and they drank in silence for a few minutes.

"It may be morbid," agreed Dad, "but that's the feeling I get, too."

Mark refrained from rolling his eyes. Why were his parents so melodramatic? Mr. Griswold was old, probably at least seventy-five, maybe older. But sometimes he acted like he was a hundred, and other times like he was twenty. But he sure didn't seem as if he was "waiting."

"I'm going to take a shower. What time are you going out?" Mark left his glass in the sink and turned to leave the kitchen.

"Around four-thirty," Mom told him. "We're going to eat out. Don't forget to call Carl."

"Okay," said Mark, as he headed toward the stairs.

*＊＊

"What did you say to him?" Maureen asked her husband.

"Nothing. Why? I told him about Yellowstone, but that was all."

"I don't know," Maureen said slowly. "He just seems so quiet."

27

"He's tired, honey. Those boys probably didn't get a wink of sleep last night." Richard also stood up. "Got to get going if I'm going to kick Silas's behind. See you at three-thirty. The course won't be crowded because everybody played early." He gave his wife a kiss on the top of her head.

"Have fun. See you later," Maureen replied. "I'll be at Mona Stringer's Bible study."

***

Mark called Carl from his parents' bedroom.

"Hey, Herb won't be here tonight. Says he's got a date." announced Carl.

"No way, not with Marcia,"

"Nah, I don't think so. He just said a date. He didn't brag or anything. Besides, it's going to take more than a day or two to even get close enough to Marcia to ask her anything. She's always surrounded by a gang of admirers."

Marcia Winkler was blond, petite, and head cheerleader at the college she attended. She'd been prom queen, class president, yearbook editor, and every other overachiever role that was possible at tiny Hemlock High. And she wore them all like a general's stars. Mark's dad once remarked she was almost too good to be true. Mark, Carl and Herb, who were enough younger not to have a chance with her, used to sit around and try to come up with one flaw in Marcia Winkler. They hadn't been successful so far.

Mark said, "Yeah, I know what you mean. Listen, I won't be there, either. Got to baby sit my sister."

"Bummer," replied Carl. "I gotta get back to work. Talk to ya later."

Chapter Three

"Hold still, Muffin," Mark scolded as the baby kicked her chubby legs and sent the pins, powder, and diaper shooting off the changing table. He placed one hand on the baby and bent to retrieve the scattered items while the baby continued to kick and squirm.

Rachael seemed like a pretty lofty name for a baby, but Mom had insisted, justifying it by stating it was a good biblical name, just as Mark was. Then she said something about mother and son and father and daughter having the same initials, yada, yada, yada. Dad had just beamed.

Rachael had not been expected. Mark had apparently been a difficult birth and the doctor had said no more children. Sometimes Mark thought doctors made pronouncements like that just to hear their heads roar. Obviously, in this case that was all it was. Rachael Murphy Stone made her appearance just before Mark's seventeenth birthday and Mark still couldn't believe he had a baby sister. All his friends had younger siblings, but they were at least able to feed themselves and wear regular clothes.

That was another thing Mom had insisted on. Cloth diapers. She said they were better for the environment, better for baby's tender skin, and better for the Stones' budget. Besides, Mom loved washing them and hanging them on the line in the sunshine.

Mark carefully refolded the diaper and quickly stuck it under the baby before she had a chance to kick it again. He only drew blood—his—once, while pinning it. Then he pulled on the green froggy waterproof diaper cover and slipped the cotton nightie over her head. He carried her to her crib and put her down next to the disreputable looking fox, her favorite toy since she could focus her eyes.

"Okay, brat. Get some sleep. I've got a date with Bill Shakespeare."

Rachael grabbed the fox's mangy tail with her left hand and stuck her right thumb in her mouth. She rolled to her side and looked up at her brother and Mark remembered why he didn't mind babysitting. He bent down and kissed the mop of brown curls. "Night night, Muffin."

"Mu mu," said Rachael.

Mark's summer would be pretty much taken up helping his father at the mortuary plus summer school. School wouldn't start for a couple of weeks, but he already had his books and assigned reading. One class was a four-week prerequisite composition course for college, and the other was a Shakespeare course that he'd signed up for in a weak moment just because Deborah Stringer had registered to take it. He couldn't back out now without looking like a jerk. And he might be able to apply it to some college credits. He was stuck taking it, but maybe he would get to study with Deborah. Yeah, right, and maybe cows could jump over the moon. Football practice wouldn't start until the end of August, so all in all, the summer loomed ahead like a long, boring road. Yellowstone was looking pretty good.

***

Back in his room Mark hauled *The Complete Works of Shakespeare* out of his knapsack and lugged the heavy book to his desk. The first assignment was "The Tempest", and the class was to have it read by the first day of school. Piece of cake.

Maybe not.

Thunder rumbled faintly in the distance. Well, great. Act 1, Scene I began with a "tempestuous noise" being heard by everyone on a ship at sea. Outside, the wind picked up and sent the smell of rain through the open window next to the desk. Mark kept his finger in the page of the overview of "The Tempest" as he continued reading.

A gust of wind sent droplets of rain across the page. Mark grabbed a dirty sock off the floor and blotted the moisture, careful not to rub and smear the ink. The thunder was becoming louder, though not quite at the booming stage yet. He'd managed to get to Scene II, trying desperately to stay awake long enough to sort out the nine characters who appeared within the first few pages.

He stood and stretched, glancing out the window at the streetlight. A bolt of lightning arced across the sky just over the Bakers' house across the street. A split second later the boom of thunder shook the windows, and the lights went out. Mark grabbed a flashlight from the desk drawer and crossed the hall to check on Rachael. Sound asleep. He pulled her light blanket over her and lowered the window slightly.

Just as he crossed the hall back to his room the lights came back on. Rats. He was hoping to have an excuse not to read any more. Oh well. Back to work. But first he went downstairs and fixed himself a large iced tea. Then he checked to make sure all the windows were secured.

"Enough stalling, Stone," Mark muttered to himself as he started back up the stairs. Another flash of lightning. Mark continued up the stairs, glancing up when he got halfway.

"Behold I stand at the door and knock."

"Wha—!" Mark's iced tea hit the wall and splattered over his face, clothes, feet and the stair tread. The plastic glass bounced down the stairs. The lights went out.

***

"Hilda, where are the candles?" Malcolm called from the kitchen.

"In the drawer by the refrigerator," replied his wife as she hastily closed windows.

"Never mind, the lights are back on."

Hilda stuck her head in. "Better get them ready just in case. It feels like this weather is going to hang around for a while."

Malcolm rummaged around and came up with four candles and four mismatched holders. He had just started toward the living room when the lights went out again.

"You were right," he mumbled as he fumbled with a match and got one of the candles lit. He placed it on the table beside Hilda's chair, then lit another and carried it to the bookcase.

Hilda looked up. "Who could that be on a night like this?"

Malcolm looked at her. "What?"

"Someone's at the door. I heard a voice."

With a slight shrug of his shoulders Malcolm walked to the door and opened it. Lightning. Thunder. A sheet of rain. Malcolm slammed the door shut. He looked at his wife closely. "You sure you haven't been in the cooking sherry?"

"Oh, land sakes, Mal," Hilda waved him away and went back to her book.

Malcolm chuckled and picked up his crossword puzzle.

***

Outside Mark's bedroom window a couple of puddles developed on the sill. Muco shouted, "Can't even get this fag lit in this God forsaken weather. Hah! Get it? God forsaken?"

Klork raked his talons down Muco's hideous face. "It seems to me you should be more concerned with who just arrived here instead of setting fire to that coffin nail," he pointed out, expanding his senses to see into Mark's bedroom. "He's heavy duty, not some numbskull like you and I. He's only one rung or so below *Michael.*"

At the name Michael, more thunder sounded, and the puddles became vapor, leaving only large drops of rain gathering on and spilling off the sill.

***

Nobody was there. Mark had managed to creep down the stairs and grab a flashlight from the hall table. But when he aimed it up the stairs there was nothing there. No one, nothing, not even a breeze coming in the upstairs hall window. He stood rooted at the foot of the stairs and waited for the blast of adrenalin to ease up. Then, on rubbery legs, he climbed slowly up toward the top of the staircase, flashlight trained on the top of the stairs. He'd heard a voice. He was certain.

Rachael!

His adrenaline kicked in again and he bolted up the last five steps in two strides, skidded down the hall, threw open his sister's door and almost dropped the flashlight in his haste to shine it into the crib.

Asleep.

Mark held on to the crib rail and fought for breath, fought for control, fought his rebellious stomach. Watching the baby's tiny chest rise and fall with each breath restored his center of gravity, and his own breathing returned to almost normal. His heart still pounded and his clothes were soaked with sweat, but everything looked normal. The walls, the mobile above the crib, the toy fox staring up at him with one eye, and most important, Rachael, sleeping the sleep of the very young.

Mark allowed himself to squat on his heels beside the crib. He took a deep breath, then another. Sitting there in the dark with only the sound of his sister's breathing, he felt a gradual calm settle over him. Rain beat against the window like billions of fingernails, crashing thunder followed each blaze of lightning. As a storm, it could have competed with William Shakespeare's. Mark felt merely peace.

Not only peace, but a sense of wellness somewhat akin to the absolute calm that followed a very rough scrimmage on the high school football field.

"Endorphins," Mark muttered to himself. "After that adrenalin rush it's a wonder I didn't have a heart attack."

That was it. The endorphins took over and calmed him down. Man, Mother Nature rocked!

Okay, smart guy, so where did the voice come from? The Jolly Green Giant?

"Nah, I didn't get enough sleep last night. Make that *any* sleep last night. And I'm trying to sort through Alonso, Sebastian, Gonzalo and who knows who else. No wonder I'm hallucinating."

Rachael stirred and sighed. Mark jumped as if he'd been jabbed with a hot needle.

"What am I doing squatting on my baby sister's bedroom floor talking to myself?"

He stood and tiptoed to the door. Stuck his head out. No one there.

"Of course not, idiot. Go to bed. Get some sleep."

Sometime during the past few minutes the lights had come back on. Mark did a careful search of the house, starting in the basement, where he armed himself with a baseball bat, wishing he hadn't seen all those *Friday the Thirteenth* movies, and checking the door to the tunnel to make sure it was locked. What had happened to that peaceful feeling he'd had in Rachael's room? But the storm was diminishing and all that remained was an occasional rumble in the distance. A shower was what he needed.

The shower alleviated some of the confusion and scenarios that were rattling around in his head like bumper cars. Thunder sometimes sounded like a thousand voices. Rain could create its own voice, beating on the roof or slanting against a window. Add that to the myriad of Shakespeare characters all scrambling to stay alive during the storm. And, of course, the fact that he was dead tired. Then he remembered he'd just had a shower before Mom and Dad left. Oh well, you can never be too clean. Besides, after tonight's adventure, he needed at least another one.

It was eleven P.M. Mark hadn't the faintest idea where the night had gone, but he was definitely ready for bed. He lay awake for a few minutes think-

35

ing about the voice he'd heard. But was it a voice or just a strong recollection? After all, Hilda had recited it just this morning.

He didn't hear his parents come home.

Chapter Four

Carl nailed the twelfth replacement plank onto the Winklers' dock. Only four to go. It hadn't been too bad this year. Last year they'd replaced twenty-two weather beaten planks and five uprights. This year was a piece of cake. He'd be finished with this dock by four o'clock.

"Catch."

Carl reached out and snagged the bottle of water Mark launched at him.

"Thanks. What are you up to?" Carl unscrewed the cap, poured half of the water over his head and drank the rest.

Mark sat down beside him. "Not much. How's Herb doing with Marcia?"

Carl snorted. "Who knows? I haven't seen either of them." He tossed his empty bottle into the nearby trash container and indicated his work. "I'm just about through with this. Tomorrow we get to start on the small one. You coming over tonight?"

Mark sat down on the finished part of the dock, drew his knees up, and took a long pull of his water. "Yeah. Thought we could torture Herb. He's never going to score with Marcia. Need help with this?"

"Nah. I'm through for the day as soon as I get the rest of these planks on. Why don't you pick up a really raunchy movie."

Mark winced as he thought of the voice at the top of the stairs the other night. No way on this green earth was he going to tell anyone, least of all Carl or Herb, about it. In fact, it seemed so unreal now that he'd almost forgotten about it. Almost.

He stood up. "Yeah, sure. I'll see what I can find. Maybe *Nightmare on*

Elm Street. I think it's part gazillion or something like that."

Carl laughed. "Excellent. It'll go with the pizza. Oh, and call Herb."

"Okay. Have a ball nailing. Later." Mark was whistling by the time he got to his car. Things were back on track.

***

"Pull, for cryin' out loud! What are you, some kind of wimp?" Klork held Muco's fins, slippery as they were, and yelled his ugly head off while Muco tried getting his claws under the loose board on Kyle Turner's bedroom floor. As demons, they were poor, underdeveloped weaklings. But they were learning. Now they were trying to get into Kyle's stash and change the bags around before Herb snuck in to help himself.

Muco stuck his serpent's head up and screeched, "Just shut your ugly pie hole. Yer yelling is enough to wake the dead." Then he chuckled at his joke. "Hahaha, get it?" He reached down between the boards, which had been pried up enough to afford a handhold, or in this case, a claw hold on the precious bags. Quickly he slid one over and put the good stuff on top.

"That should do it," he muttered to himself as he heaved himself back, sending Klork skittering across the room.

Both started as footsteps began pounding up the stairs. By the time Herb was at the doorway there was no sign of anything amiss.

***

The Video Store didn't have the 1987 *Nightmare on Elm Street,* so Mark settled for *Jaws: The Revenge.*

They ate pizza and tried to watch the movie while Herb regaled them with his plan for capturing the heart of Marcia Winkler.

"See, I figure she's been home for a week now, and there's nothing going on. The centennial isn't until the end of July, so even if she's working on that float, there's not that much to do yet."

Mark tried his "Shut up" routine a couple of times but that didn't help. Finally Carl stood up and poured his Coke over Herb's head. That settled their friend down for a while.

Later, they lay on top of their sleeping bags in the boathouse, watching the smoke from their shared reefer curl lazily toward the ceiling. The Grateful Dead was telling the world that they would survive. Thankfully, Herb was too stoned to talk much. That wouldn't last, but for now silence reigned. Mark had his headache back, right on schedule. He was beginning to wonder about his sanity, his sense, and his survival.

"So, who'd you go out with Sunday?" Carl to Herb.

"Uh, Sunday." Herb being stupid. "Let's see, so many girls . . ."

"Fer crying out loud, Turner, you just ain't that much of a lady killer. With that sunburn you've got a face like a ripe mango. Who'd you take out Sunday?"

"All right, all right, Jessica, okay?"

"Jessica Washburn? No way, dude! She's a toothpick! How'd you hold on?" Carl, the crude.

Herb had the decency to look sheepish. "We just went to a ball game. Her little brother was playing. Then we went for ice cream."

Carl sighed, took a drag, passed the butt to Mark, and said, "That's no date, man. That's an After School Special. Yeesh, I thought you had a date. Maybe you *better* get together with Marcia. You just might be hopeless."

Mark inserted a toothpick in the last half-inch of the joint and took a drag. Whoa! Right into his brain. Not so bad, after all. "Yeah, Turner, Jessica makes Popeye's Olive Oil look like Jabba the Hutt."

Herb rushed to his own defense. "All right, Ma made me go. It was a mercy date."

"You got that right," replied Mark as he took another cigarette paper Carl extended and expertly started assembling a second joint. Hilda's words washed over him again. *Don't let anyone talk . . .*

"I happen to know that Marcia is working at the library this summer," announced Herb, happy for the opportunity to leave the Jessica subject. "I really need to get a library card. Thought I'd stop in Monday."

Both boys reacted. "You don't have a library card?" Carl slowly shook his head.

"Man, you're pitiful. No wonder you date people like Jessica Washburn," Mark continued as he sealed the paper around the weed. "Everybody's got a library card. I think even my little sister's got a library card. They're like social security cards. You *gotta* have a library card."

Herb's face was now the color of a ripe persimmon. "Okay! So everybody's got one. I just never got around to it. I always used Ma's."

Carl rolled his eyes. "And you're—how old?"

Mark spoke up. "Hey, guys, speaking of mothers, my mom needs a few people to help cook and serve chicken on the 28th, opening day of the Centennial.

40

It's a Friday and I've still got school. I, um, sort of volunteered you—".

"What?" in unison from his friends.

Mark held his hands up, reefer carefully balanced between two of his fingers, "—but only until I get there. No later than two."

"Oh man," grumbled Herb, embarrassment forgotten. "I'll smell like fried chicken for the rest of the summer."

"Better than what you smell like now," Carl observed, and laughed at his own joke.

Herb ignored him.

"Hey, I can't help it if the Centennial starts the last day of summer school," Mark said. "Besides, what are friends for?" He ducked as Herb launched an empty coke can at him.

"Quit! I'll be there at two! Promise."

"Yeah, and what if I have a date with Marcia?" Herb.

Carl did another eye roll. "Not a chance."

Mark ignored Herb. "Good. Then it's settled. I'll tell Mom that my two *best friends* are going to help out." He waved off the joint when it was his turn. One lousy rush, that was it. His headache was back full throttle, his guilt was beginning to rear its ugly head, and the room felt like a peat bog.

They were quiet for a while. Mark was almost asleep when one of the sleeping bags came to life.

"It stinks in here," mumbled Herb as he shuffled across the room and opened a window.

"Open all of them. We need to air the place out. My parents don't come up here much, but with our luck they'll decide to have their next dinner party up here." Carl stood, picked up a corner of his sleeping bag and sniffed it, recoiling from the smell that greeted him. "Yuck. How many of those things did we have? Place smells worse than a rock concert."

Mark thought about it. Tried to think about it. His brain didn't want to engage. He preferred watching Carl pick up his sleeping bag in slow motion, un-zip it in slow motion, and spread it out on the floor in front of the open windows. In slow motion. Heck of a show.

"Hey, Stone, you in there?" Herb was holding a bag of marijuana in one hand and waving his other hand in front of Mark's face.

"Yeah. How many? Uh, t-two, I think."

"Oh, man, I brought the wrong bag. This stuff is 'OFF LIMITS'!" Kyle said." Herb looked around in desperation, as if a guardian angel might material-ize and save him. "Actually, I snuck it. He doesn't know I have any at all."

"So, what's so off limits about this?" Carl asked, squinting at the plastic bag Herb was now holding like a live grenade.

"It's got the good stuff in it. Man, he's gonna kill me."

This was beginning to be fun. Mark had said they were going to torture Herb, but the neat thing now was that he was torturing himself. All Mark and Carl had to do was sit back and watch the spectacle. Awesome, The only problem Mark was having was staying awake.

"Hey, Stone, take me home," Herb demanded, jamming the bag in his knapsack and grabbing his shoes.

"What? What are you talkin' about? It's only midnight. I don't know about you, but I believe it's either too early or too late to go home. Either way, I'm not taking you." Mark slid further down into his sleeping bag, ignoring the sickly sweet smell of cannabis.

"C'mon, man. We can come right back. Kyle gets off work at midnight. He'll be home any minute. If I can get this stuff back there before he gets home, maybe he won't notice any missing."

Carl came back from shaking his sleeping bag out the window. "Yeah, man, take him home. I'll air out your bags while you're gone. If Kyle finds out about this we'll be in a mess of trouble.

Don't let anyone talk you into anything.

"Yeah, but this is different."

"Huh?"

Mark looked up to see his friends watching him as if he'd just spoken Swahili. Then he realized he'd spoken to Hilda. It was pretty obvious Hilda wasn't in the boathouse.

He'd heard the words as if they'd been spoken to him just now. *But it wasn't Hilda's voice.*

Mark had to think fast. Unfortunately, Mark wasn't capable of thinking at all right now. He sat up and took a deep breath. Mistake. He felt like he'd inhaled every bit of smoke left in the boathouse. He coughed once, cleared his throat, and since thinking fast was out of the question, he thought hard.

Herb and Carl continued to stare.

"Uh, okay. Hillman, you take Herb home and I'll air out the sleeping bags." Mark pulled his keys out of his shoe and tossed them to a startled Carl.

"What? You never let anybody even *touch* your car. What's up with that?" Carl asked with more than a little suspicion in his voice.

Mark gave him the best smile he could come up with—something between a snarl and a gape—and replied, "Call me Mr. Nice Guy." Then he added, "I don't feel like driving. I'd rather stay here and air out the bags. You can thank me later."

He grabbed his sleeping bag and gave Herb a shove, pitching him over onto his side, where he continued tying his shoes. "Man, you're sure acting weird," his friend observed as he stood and picked up his knapsack.

Meanwhile Mark, intent on his mission, started unzipping and shaking out the sleeping bags, keeping his back to the other two and whistling quietly through his teeth. Carl and Herb stood watching him for a minute. Then Herb shrugged and mouthed, "Let's go," to Carl.

Carl said to Mark, "There's a fan in the closet if you think it would help." Mark nodded but said nothing. Carl took the can containing the residual from the evening's activities, to pitch into an unsuspecting dumpster, and the two of them left. They went quietly down the outside stairs of the boathouse and walked as soundlessly as possible to Mark's car, which was parked on the opposite side of the house from Carl's parents' bedroom.

Once in the car Herb blew out his breath in a whoosh and said slowly, "What is going on with our friend? Has he lost his marbles, or is it just the funny cigarettes? Man, he's spooky."

Carl started the car and listened to the engine purr for a while, savoring the sweet sound and wondering how he'd managed to get so lucky tonight. Then he remembered the tension in Mark's shoulders and the set to his jaw as he'd tried to act casual. Maybe it *was* the pot. Maybe he was one of those people who don't react well to it. Then he mentally kicked himself . React well? He'd been to the classes, heard his own father, for Pete's sake, lecture on the dangers of marijuana. Just because it was easy to come by, relatively cheap, and everybody did it, didn't make it any less a mood-altering drug—an *illegal* mood-altering drug.

Carl became aware that Herb was talking to him. ". . . least he had the sense to know not to drive. Maybe it's some sort of allergy."

"Turner, you are such a jerk. You don't have to be allergic to a drug to react to it. Pot is a heavy-duty *drug*." Carl put the car in gear and backed slowly into the street. He prayed that no one would hear them leave, keeping the headlights off until they were safely away from the house. He prayed *hard* that none of his father's cronies would spot them cruising through the back streets, carrying an unknown quantity of weed in a plastic sack.

***

Carl Senior, who went by his middle name, Philip, was chief of police of Hemlock, Missouri. After two tours in Viet Nam, there was very little that surprised or scared him. Now he stood at the kitchen window and watched the Nova move down the street, headlights off, like a thief. He shook his head. Didn't anybody know that was one of the quickest ways to draw attention? Where was Mark going at this hour?

***

Back at the boathouse, Mark placed the tiny electric fan on the windowsill, facing out. Then he carried the sleeping bags outside and spread them
45

out along the dock. It was pitch black. Everyone in the neighborhood was asleep so there was no danger of being seen. The only way to get the smell out of the bags, short of washing them, was to expose them to as much fresh air as possible. The three of them weren't going to get much sleep anyhow, and who knew when the other two were going to get back.

***

"Didn't I tell you he's going to the other side?" Muco shrieked at his co-hort.

"I don't think a simple act of airing out the place and acting self-righteous for a brief period of time constitutes a complete crossover," Klork hissed in response. "Our time would be better spent sabotaging that chapel on the beach." Muco grabbed his companion's skinny arm and dragged him away.

***

The tiny hairs on the back of Mark's neck stood to attention. What was that? It sounded like someone screaming, just for a split second. He whirled around, nearly losing his balance and landing in the water. From his vantage point it looked like two shadows were locked in mortal combat. What? Shadows? *You're losing it, Mark. You're marbles are going to the dark side and taking your brain with them.*

Mark closed his eyes and shook his head. Did he have permanent brain damage? It was very possible. No telling what Kyle's stuff had been laced with.

He walked over and looked down at the ground where he'd seen the two shadows. Nothing. Just some dust settling from the faint breeze that came off the lake. He thought he detected a whiff of sulfur. "Nah, just my nose trying to adjust to fresh air."

Mark stood on the dock for ten minutes looking out over the lake. He could just see the light in front of the Barbour cabin directly across the water, a distance of just under a mile. Their nearest neighbors, the Winklers, had one light on but were otherwise down for the night. Waves lapped at the shore in peaceful harmony with the crickets and all was still.

Something told him it wasn't the pot that had caused the vision, as he chose to call it. But something was happening to him, and he felt propelled along by an unseen force. Mark made his way back up the stairs to check the progress of the airing out. It could have been worse. He rummaged around under the sink in the bathroom and found a rusted can of air freshener. Standing in the middle of the room, he aimed the can toward the ceiling and turned slowly in a circle as he sprayed. Now the boathouse smelled like pot and cinnamon. Oh well, he supposed it could be mistaken for cheap aftershave.

***

Hilda sat up and looked at the luminous dial on the clock. Twelve thirty-seven. She and Malcolm had been in bed two hours. Normally Hilda slept soundly until three or four A.M. when Henry, their large, orange, mixed breed dog came over and licked her face. She would get up and take him out, bring him back in, go to the bathroom, come back to bed and go back to sleep without coming fully awake.

Henry was sound asleep in his bed on the floor next to Malcolm, who was snoring quietly. Something else had awakened her. What? She looked around the tiny bedroom, lit only by the clock dial and the night light next to the door. It was

47

a moonless night and the only outside light was in the front.

Where had that come from? Oh, good grief, was she beginning to hear voices? No, it hadn't been a voice; it was more a knowing, or a feeling, than the actual spoken word. Exactly like last week during the thunderstorm. She had written that off as "Things that go bump in the night."

Now, though, there was no storm, no extraneous sounds from within or without. What had awakened her?

Pray for Mark.

***

Carl circled the block for the third time. Still no sign of Herb. They had arrived just as Kyle was pulling into the driveway. Herb had jumped out and said something about coming back for more tapes, turned and whispered to Carl to circle the block four times, and had followed his brother into the house.

"Okay, smart guy, this is it," mumbled Carl as he started the last turn around the block.

The front door opened and Herb came hurtling down the steps. Tearing across the lawn, he opened the car door and threw himself in. "Go!"

"What is this, a bank robbery? You've been watching too many cheesy Saturday matinees." Carl did step on it as he rounded the corner and headed back toward the lake. "How did it go?"

Herb, slightly out of breath, glanced into the side mirror. "I thought he was headed for the shower. I went in his room and started to pull the floorboard off—that's where he keeps his stash—and I heard him in the hall." He paused for a breath. "I quick threw the bag in. I didn't even put it in the right place, fer cryin' out loud. Then I threw the floorboard back and snuck through the door between our rooms. Thank God there's a door there, or my—"

"So you're clear. So, what's the problem?" Carl was getting a little tired of the high drama.

"Man, he'll kill me if he suspects I've even been *in* his room! I don't understand how I got the wrong bag. They were arranged exactly the way they were last time. Kyle never rearranges them." Beads of sweat appeared on Herb's upper lip and Carl fought the urge to smack him.

"Look. Even if something's out of place, he can't *prove* anything. Especially since there's hardly anything gone from that bag. What? Two joints worth? He'll just think he got them mixed up." Carl turned the car down the lake road that led to his house. "Just don't do it again, okay? You—*we*—could get in a *mess* of trouble that way. Not for stealing your brother's stash, but we could have gotten picked up for driving around in Mark's car in the middle of the night with all the evidence."

They pulled in where Mark had parked the car earlier, so no one would notice it had been moved. Mark met them at the dock. "Grab your bags. They're as aired out as I could get them." He had sprayed the upstairs again and now it smelled like the gym on prom night instead of basketball finals.

"How do you feel?" asked Herb, as they began spreading out their sleeping bags one more time.

Mark resisted the urge to say, "with my hands," and settled for, "Good. Great. Guess I just needed a little fresh air."

***

Philip finished his second glass of ice water standing at the kitchen window in the dark. He was just making up his mind to go look for the boys when Mark's car pulled back in. Good. At least he was safe. Then Herb and Carl got out, Carl out of the driver's side. Not good. He set the glass by the sink and took the stairs two at a time. Pulling on a pair of sweats and a t-shirt, he stuffed his feet into his tennies and headed for the stairs again.

"Phil? What is it?" his wife's muffled voice came from the bed.

"Not sure, Hon, I'm just going to check on the boys. Be right back."

Pam sat up. "I'll come with you." She threw back the covers and reached for the bedside lamp.

"It's okay." Phil took his wife's shoulders and lowered her back down. "They're all right. A couple of them just went for an unscheduled drive. I'm going to find out why. Stay here."

Pam yawned. "All right. Hurry back." She was asleep before he reached the bottom of the stairs.

Phil knew the walk to the boathouse as well as he knew the walk from the dining room to the kitchen. He could navigate it with his eyes closed, pretty much like tonight, which was moonless and dark as the inside of a well. He had a flashlight but didn't turn it on.

"Hey, Carl!"

The boys froze.

"Dad," whispered Carl, needlessly.

Six seconds ticked by.

Footsteps on the stairs. "Boys!"

"Go, go, go," urged Mark, pushing Carl toward the door.

Approximately seven hundred possibilities, none of them good, careened through Carl's mind as he turned the knob and opened the door. His last thought before he confronted his father—his *cop* father—was to wipe that guilty look off his face and remain calm.

One out of two wasn't bad. He thought his face may possibly have been wiped clean of any expression save mild curiosity as his heart thundered in his chest, probably bulging out the front of his t-shirt with each beat. Thank goodness it was dark.

His Dad stopped halfway up the stairs. "What's going on? I saw you leave and come back with Mark's car."

"Oh, yeah." *How could he have seen them? He was supposed to be asleep! On the other side of the house!*

Okay, think fast, smart guy.

Mark and Herb stood just inside the door just behind Car. Mark whispered to Herb, "You wanted to go home and borrow some tapes from Kyle. He just got off work." He gave Herb a shove.

"H-hi, Mr. Hillman. I had to go home to borrow some tapes from my brother. He, uh, won't let me in his room so I had to wait until he got off work," Herb managed to state without too much stammering.

Carl picked up the thread. "I wanted to drive Mark's car. Figured it was late enough, there wouldn't be too much traffic."

A regular little choirboy.

Philip nodded slightly and appraised the three boys standing there in the

51

doorway. Not a lot of fidgeting. Fairly good eye contact. Eyes a little too wide and innocent. Hmmm.

"May I come in?" he asked politely, taking a step toward them.

Ohmygosh.

"Sure," in unison, as the boys stepped aside.

Flashlights circled the sleeping bags like wagons at an Indian massacre. Phil flicked on his own torch and gave the area his cop's once over. Clean at first glance. Nothing out of place, no lumps or bumps in the sleeping bags—which would have indicated booze or girls. The smell, well, it smelled like Pam's air freshener. The cinnamon one that gave him a headache. Now why would they be spraying air freshener around at midnight?

Phil decided to focus on the immediate. He looked at Mark, who looked a little pale, even in the flashlight glow. "As far as I know, son, your father is not carrying Carl on his auto insurance policy. Is that correct?"

Mark maintained his air of innocence and replied, "No, sir. I mean yes, sir. Uh—that's correct."

Carl piped up with, "It's my fault, Dad. I begged and pleaded. He had a headache anyway, so I thought it would be better if I drove." A candidate for canonization.

Phil could certainly understand why Mark had a headache. His own head was beginning to pound from the stink of the air freshener. Wait. Was that what he smelled? Yes, but that wasn't all. The cloying, sickening smell characteristic of burning cannabis practically slapped him in the face, once he mentally set aside the cutesy country charm of the cinnamon. It wasn't recent, as in hastily extinguished as he came up the stairs. But it was sometime tonight, with most of the evidence gone, no doubt. That's probably what the midnight ride had been about.

Disappointment jabbed through him as he realized he'd fooled himself into believing he had the perfect family. Perfect wife, perfect kids, perfect job, perfect life. Bull.

Phil gave himself a mental shake and forced himself to stick to the subject. The rest he'd address later.

He turned to his son, who looked like he'd swallowed a live snake. "Do not drive anybody's car except ours. I pay Allstate a bucketful of money just for the privilege of worrying my socks off every time you get behind the wheel. Do *not*," he repeated, "drive Mark's car, or your sister's car, or your girlfriend's car, or Grandpa's car."

Carl almost fainted with relief. That's what this was about. The car. They were safe! He didn't suspect anything! Carl felt like sitting down just to get off his wobbly knees. Beside him, he could hear Mark and Herb breathing as if they'd been holding their collective breath for about a week.

Carl remembered to say, "Yes, sir," and to look properly chastised.

Dad gave the room one more glance, instructed, "Get some sleep. No more midnight drives," and walked out. The boys almost dislocated their respective shoulders high-fiving each other.

Chapter Five

Why was he awake at 7 a.m.? School wasn't until ten and here he was wide awake. What made it worse was it was raining. Perfect sleeping weather, and here he was awake and ready to start the day. In the summer, 7 a.m. wasn't even civilized.

He could hear his mother talking to Rachael, and the baby making inarticulate drooling sounds that can only be interpreted by mothers and the family dog. Mark lay on his back and stared at the ceiling for a few minutes, and then got up and pulled on his shorts. On the plus side was the fact that he wouldn't have to mow Hilda and Malcolm's grass today. Instead, he could wander over to the library and, quite by chance, just happen to run into Deborah and maybe, just maybe, sit at the same table to study.

Pathetic.

Just as he opened the bedroom door he thought he heard a voice. He glanced in the mirror over his dresser. Nah, his imagination. Mark went down and joined Mom and Rachael for an early breakfast.

Sometimes the very best plans don't exactly pan out. The rain stopped by eight o'clock and everything was dry by eleven. By the time Mark was through with his comp class he knew there'd be no trip to the library for him. Bummer. Between helping Dad, studying, writing compositions, and actual school time, he not only hadn't seen his best friends for more than five minutes at a time, he hadn't gotten past the hello stage with Deborah. Shakespeare was more than half over. They had *King Lear* to finish and *As You Like It* after that. The Centennial started the last day of summer school which, in Mark's opinion, was poor planning on the part of everybody. That would certainly muddy the water as far as trying to find a moment alone with Deborah, and Mark wasn't exactly Don Juan in the romance department. Now he had to move fast. He was worse than Herb, who'd at least gotten to drive Marcia home from the library one day. It hadn't been a date, but it was something, even though the end of June had come and gone and he'd lost his bet.

***

"Don't bother trying; you'll fail."

It sounded almost conversational. The only problem was Hilda was alone in the kitchen. In fact, she was alone in the cabin. Malcolm had gone to St. Louis to an antique books convention and wouldn't be home until Sunday night. Henry the dog was outside getting as muddy as he possibly could before coming back in to shake his heavy coat all over the veggie print wallpaper.

Hilda carefully set down her rolling pin and turned around. The front door was open and rain was spattering across the floor. She quickly went over and glanced out to be sure no one was there. She shut the door, and then mopped up the water with a kitchen towel.

"It must have blown open, "she muttered to herself, and went back to rolling out pie dough.

A scream. Faint but unmistakable, and cut off as suddenly as it started. She clutched the rolling pin and walked to the kitchen door. Opened it. Henry was sleeping on the porch. He lifted his head and yawned.

"C'mon, Henry. You can protect me."

Henry lumbered to his feet, shook himself, spraying water to the four corners of the porch and drenching Hilda, and shambled inside. Nothing in his demeanor indicated anything but a nap in the rain. Obviously the dog hadn't experienced any disturbance any time lately.

Hilda got a large towel from the dog basket in the corner of the bedroom and began rubbing Henry, who sat down and licked her face, tail continuing to distribute droplets everywhere. "So, you didn't hear a thing, huh?"

The tail-wag revved up a notch.

"Didn't think so." Hilda finished drying the dog as best she could and stood up. Henry gave a mighty shake and finished the job. Then he turned around twice and lay down on the throw rug to continue his nap.

***

"What was *that* supposed to accomplish?" Muco bellowed at his companion as they splattered around in a mud puddle next to the kitchen porch. He'd been trying to light up his smoke and hadn't been successful. Now he threw the thing down in frustration. "You know we're not supposed to do the auditory thing until we've been checked out on it. And that requires a stack of forms and seventeen signatures."

"Stop that ridiculous blathering," hissed Klork, trying desperately to stand up in the muck and finally sliding onto his seat, his spiny tail sending up a plume of water onto the porch recently vacated by Henry. "She actually heard it! From here! Woo! What a rush!"

Muco fished another cancer stick out of his voluminous cloak and hunched over as he attempted to light it. This time he succeeded, and he blew a cloud of sulfurous smoke in his companion's face. Then he screamed, "That's not

56

the point! What if someone from the home office found out? They'd take us out of here and make us do some *real* work!"

Klork inhaled deeply of the acrid smoke and slithered to his feet. "No one will find out. They don't care about us. All we need to do is get that kid on the wrong track and we can go home . . ."

"Don't be too sure," screeched Muco, as he wrapped his cloak around himself and prepared to vaporize. "I feel as if we're being watched."

"You're being paranoid again," purred Klork as he followed the screeching apparition into the ether.

***

The rain stopped. Hilda finished her pies and packed and labeled them. By early afternoon she had weeded, walked her two miles, and straightened the kitchen. Now she sat down and opened her Bible to John's Gospel.

In the beginning was the Word, and the Word was with God, and the Word was God. He was in the beginning with God.

The sound of the lawnmower startled Hilda out of her concentration. She sat for a while and just listened to what was being communicated to her. Finally she nodded to herself, knowing she had received the answer she was seeking.

***

Mark's mood was getting darker by the minute as he grimly mowed straight rows between the logs in front of the cabin. He'd finished the Barbours' grass at their house in town and was backing out of their driveway in time to see Deborah go by in a strange car with a strange guy at the wheel. He ground his teeth when, just as the car came past, Deborah leaned over and planted a kiss on

57

the guy's cheek. What! Right out in public! She kissed him! They hadn't seen him backing out of the driveway and they drove merrily off while Mark sat there for a minute, contemplating the summer in general, and his life in particular. Both totally messed up.

Bummer.

Hilda met him on the porch with a tall glass of lemonade, which he gratefully accepted.

"How are you getting along with Mr. Shakespeare?" she inquired, noting the unhappy look in his eyes.

"Okay. It's nearly over," Mark answered, not wanting to be rude, but really wanting to just leave. He drank his lemonade.

"I'll bet you're ready. You can enjoy the centennial."

"Yeah, it'll be a relief to have school over with. Football practice starts the third week in August. Dad wants to take us to Yellowstone, but I don't know how we'll fit it in." Mark finished his lemonade and Hilda took the glass.

"Mark, come in here for a minute. There's something I want to give you," Hilda said as she walked back into the cabin.

Mark stole a look at his watch. Four o'clock. There was still time to cruise around before he had to go home and help Dad. Maybe he could find that car Deb was in. Oh, great, Stone. Then what? Zap it with your Super-death-deliverer-fazer gun? That would certainly work.

The cabin, though not air conditioned, managed to stay cool even in the summer, thanks to the huge Sycamores that practically surrounded it. Mark took a deep breath of the cool, cinnamon-laden air, and felt a little of the negative effects of the day lift slightly. Hilda could do that to him. "Now, I know you're up to your chin in reading this summer," she told him, "but that's why I chose now, while you're in that mode. I want you to look it over. You don't have to read it cover to cover, just get a feel for it. It's not a read cover-to-cover book." She held a book out to him and added, "Humor an old lady. You have nothing to lose. God is in this with us, I know it."

Mark's eyes strayed to the picture hanging over the bookcase as he reached out to take the book. When he looked back at Hilda she had tears in her own eyes. For whatever reason, Mark suddenly thought about the voices he heard—thought he heard, and that sense of calm came over him again. "I will. Look at it. Y-you don't mind if I wait until after Shakespeare, do you?" Then, suddenly bold, he asked, "Why me?"

Oh, no, had he hurt her feelings?

Hilda smiled. "Why not you? I've known you all your life, Mark. I watched you grow from a toddler, to a little boy, to a young teen who could barely start the mower. You're special to me. Besides, this is what I do. But I'll not be pressuring you." She reached out and briefly touched his arm. "God bless you. Let me know how it goes."

Mark nodded, at such a loss for words that he didn't have the faintest idea what to do next. He heard himself stammer a few syllables that may have been akin to thanks and backed out the door. Hilda stood and watched as he walked to his car.

***

"Mark, is that you?" his mother called from the kitchen. "Carl wants you

59

to call him. Then go help your dad. He's trying to get that carpet dry before the viewing tonight."

Mom appeared, carrying the fan from the family room. "Here, take this— are you all right?"

"Yeah, why?" Mark gave her a quizzical look as he took the fan from her.

"You just look different. Did you get a haircut? No, I can see you didn't." She frowned slightly and put her hand on his forehead.

"Ma, I'm fine," Mark persisted as he backed away.

"Are you sure you didn't get overheated? It's been so hot—"

Mark began laughing.

"Ma, I promise there's nothing wrong with me. I'm great. Never better." he insisted.

The truth was he *did* feel great. He didn't know why, but he felt better than he had all summer.

"Well, all right," Maureen said slowly, watching him with a mother's critical eye. "If you're sure."

"I'm sure. I'll take this to Dad." Carrying the fan, Mark made his escape and walked the short distance to the funeral home. As he passed the mirror in the entryway he glanced at himself, just to be sure. Same crop of light red hair, now bleached nearly white, same slightly sunburned nose, now peeling, same ice blue eyes, the ones his mother said would melt some girl's heart someday with their intensity. Well, they could start any time now, specifically with Deborah. Like that was going to happen in this lifetime.

His mood began to plummet again as he thought about that kiss. Who was he? Mark knew nearly every kid in the county and a bunch from the surrounding area. But he couldn't place this guy. Wonderful. First voices, and now this jerk, who got himself kissed by Deb.

Mark went into the office and used the phone to call Carl. Carl's mother answered. "Hi, Mark. Carl's outside. I'll get him. Have you talked to him lately?"

"No, ma'am, I've had school and been helping my dad. Just Fourth of July at the lakefront." The Fourth had been toned down this year because of the upcoming centennial celebration. "And I have lawns to mow on weekends," Mark replied. Why was she asking whether they'd talked? Paranoia reared its ugly head.

"Oh, I knew I hadn't seen you lately. Are you having a good summer, or are you too busy?" she asked in that friendly, candid manner that she had.

Mark gave himself a nanosecond to decide she was just making conversation. "Pretty good. It's going fast, though."

"Oh, tell me about it. The centennial will be here before we know it. Just a sec and I'll get Carl." Mark heard the phone hit a surface and Pam's voice calling Carl.

"Hullo?" Carl, sounding slightly out of breath.

"Hey, what's going on?" Mark asked.

"Have you seen Herb lately?"

"Uh, no. Why?"

"Man, he's really weirded out on us. He's hangin' with Parsons and those dudes." Carl sounded as though he couldn't quite believe it.

"What do you mean 'hangin'"?" Mark asked. "You don't mean he's doing that stuff, do you?" It was a well-known fact that those people did a lot more than pot.

"Yeah. Kate's home for a couple weeks before she goes to Branson for the rest of the summer. She was out with her boyfriend Gary the other night and he asked her if we weren't friends anymore. You know, the three of us. She says she thought so, why, and he says he sees Herb all the time with Parsons and Walker and them." Carl paused for a breath.

"Hey, wait, wait, wait," Mark cut in before Carl could continue. "Where does boyfriend Gary get off talkin' about us like we're chopped liver or something?"

"I don't know. Listen, if Herb's doing that other stuff, that means he's gonna get busted when football practice starts. And if he's hanging out with those guys, he's gonna be in deep —"

"Maybe he's just trying to get close to Marcia. Maybe she does that stuff, too." Mark thought about that. What a waste. Do that for a girl? No way. On second thought, Marcia wouldn't do that. She hung out with Deb's crowd. They didn't do anything as far as Mark knew, except go Hilda's church and that Bible study with Deborah's mother, his mother, and a bunch of other ladies.

Apparently Carl agreed. "Why would he do that? Ain't no girl worth it."

"See what else you can find out. I'll just happen to drop by his house tomorrow. You know, to rag him about the fact that he didn't score with Marcia by the end of June and when can we expect our payoff?" And find out who the rat was that Deborah was seeing seriously enough to kiss in his car in broad daylight. "You want to get together tomorrow night? Maybe I can use that as an excuse for

62

stopping by, and I can ask him if he wants to join us. If he really is hanging with those guys, it'll put him on the spot."

"Yeah, okay. I'll clear it with my parents. It's good we lay low for the past few weeks. I think my dad suspects something." Carl's voice got very quiet, as if someone were listening. "I'll tell you about it later." He hung up.

Suspected something? What? How? They hadn't even been together since the night Herb brought the wrong bag to the boathouse, and even then they'd cleaned everything up and aired it out. Mark's heart began a slow thud in his chest as he went over every detail of that night. Other than getting busted for the car episode, he couldn't think of a thing that would get Mr. Hillman's attention. The sleeping bags were all safely back upstairs, the can of residual stuff had been taken away, and the room had been aired out and even sprayed.

That was it. The air freshener. What would a bunch of teenage slobs be doing with a can of air freshener in the middle of the night? *Cinnamon* air freshener? Well, any air freshener, for that matter. Oh, man, what a stupid move that had been. Carl's dad was no fool. He'd notice the smell and probably put two and two together and . . .nah, he wouldn't have noticed. He's a guy.

Yeah, but he's a cop!

Richard found his son standing in the office holding the fan and talking to himself. "Who's a cop?" he asked, taking the fan from Mark.

"Oh, hey, Dad. Um, I was just thinking about renting *Beverly Hills Cop II* again. It was really good." The lie rolled off his tongue with no effort at all on his part.

"It was," Dad laughed. "Eddie Murphy is a funny man. Come on in here and help me move these chairs back. The carpet's just about dry, but I need to get a fan on the area in front of the casket."

Dad insisted on doing his own carpet cleaning. He maintained he could do a better job than the professionals, and he didn't want a bunch of people with hoses tramping through the place. Not that the carpets got that dirty. But they were all light-colored, so even a little soil showed up. Today, unfortunately, Richard had had to deal with a spill. Some lady at last night's visitation had been carrying an entire bottle of Pepto Bismol in her purse and it had fallen to the pale green carpet, dumping its contents across the aisle between the front rows of chairs. Dad had spent much of the day getting the putrid pink out of the pale green. No, Mark definitely did not want to follow in his dad's footsteps. The Army beckoned, looking better and better with every passing day. The college courses he was taking would help toward qualifying him for working toward a degree while he was in.

If he and his friends didn't get busted for possession, and sent to the slammer for the rest of their miserable lives.

Chapter Six

"King Lear" was depressing. There was no other way to put it. The dude had three daughters, thought two were good and one was bad. Turns out two were *real* bad and one was good. But the poor guy was deluded into thinking otherwise and ended up going insane. That was it in a nutshell. What a waste.

After school, Mark headed over to Herb's house to see what he could find out, without appearing to be trying to find out anything. He'd already seen Deborah take off with some of her friends, so he missed his big, "Hello," which he had been practicing in front of the mirror at home. He pulled up in front of the Turner house just as Herb's brother Kyle was coming down the steps. Kyle waved and came toward the car.

"Hey, you going to join us for the festivities next week?" he asked as Mark got out of the car.

"I don't know. What festivities?" Mark asked, feeling like some sort of loser outsider.

Kyle headed to his car which was parked in the driveway. "Ask Herb. We're getting a gang together to start the centennial right," Kyle replied as he jumped into his car and started it. He waved as he backed out and headed up the street.

Huh.

Mark stood on the porch waiting for someone to open the door, and wondering how he'd gotten so far out of the loop. The summer was flying by, and even though it was only half over, every minute from now on was filled, or about to be filled. Last night after he had talked to Carl, he'd eaten a quick supper and then gone up to his room to study. King Lear was trying to figure out why his daughter Goneril was treating him so badly, and Goneril was trying to get rid of all her father's knights. Thank goodness for *Cliff's Notes*.

His mind slid to the book Hilda had given him to read.

What was he thinking? He had a quiz on *King Lear* first thing in the morning and here he was, up to his elbows in . . . whatever this was. Get over it, Stone. You've got enough to do.

"Hi, Mark," the small person who opened the door greeted him. "Haven't seen you in, like, forever. Herb's in his room exterminating the Gorgoloks from the planet Drucobin. Gak!" Herb's 8-year-old little sister Heather rolled her eyes and returned to the den, where two of her friends were seated in front of a huge mirror applying a frightening amount of makeup. Either they were trying for glamour, or they were going for Bozo the Clown.

Mark could hear some serious zapping, pinging and swooping coming from behind Herb's closed bedroom door as he ascended the stairs. Ignoring the sign bearing a picture of a grumpy-looking alien which said, *"Beware, Earthlings, a slow and agonizing death awaits all who enter here,"* he pushed open the door and watched Herb finish off the Gorgoloks. "Gotcha, you scum-sucking bottom feeders!" his friend cried out in unearthly glee.

"I can't believe I actually admit I know you," said Mark from the doorway.

"Dude! Where ya been all summer?" Herb pushed back from his desk and shut down the video game. "Man, that Shakespeare must be the pits. I tried calling a couple of times, but your mom said you were either in school or mowing lawns. Bummer."

As he spoke, Herb made a half-hearted attempt at rearranging some of the mess that covered everything from bed to dresser to bookcase and the entire floor area between. "Have a seat," he invited, sweeping a pile of tapes off the only other chair. His movements were quick, jerky, almost as if he were embarrassed. Herb was never embarrassed.

Mark sat down, careful not to step on what could have been a pile of dirty laundry—or clean laundry. It was hard to tell. "So, Carl and I were thinking maybe we should get together tonight and you could give us our ten bucks—apiece— that you owe us." Mark went for the throat. "You haven't forgotten you failed to score a date with the lovely Miss Winkler by the end of June?" He leaned forward and looked his friend squarely in the eye. And had all he could do not to gasp out loud.

Bloodshot did not even begin to describe Herb's eyes. There was so little white showing that for a moment Mark seriously thought they were hemorrhaging. He forced himself to look away and take a deep breath. When he looked back, Herb was busy straightening his bed.

"Oh, yeah, that. I hadn't forgotten. I just haven't seen you guys," Herb replied quickly. He abandoned the bed and sat back down at his desk.

"But, you know, I came so close. I really think she was gonna say yes, and then Rob Morgan came along. Man, he's such a sleaze. What does he have that makes girls go all funny around him?" He carefully avoided meeting Mark's eyes again.

"You mean besides a body like a linebacker, a year-round tan, and more money than the government?" Mark offered. "Never mind he doesn't have a brain or any chance of getting one any time soon. When your daddy is a bank president and your mama is the daughter of a senator it really doesn't matter." Mark was pretty sure he was on target with his description of the spoiled-rotten senior. "He's pretty fried, but the girls don't seem to notice. Or care." Rob had been slowly destroying himself with drugs and booze since seventh grade. But he'd managed to keep in shape through three years of high school. He'd gotten kicked off the football team and some of his stunning good looks were starting to wear away. But he still had girls following him.

"Yeah, well," Herb sighed, "I hear he's going off to boarding school. It's just a rumor, but it could be true. His parents have the bucks, that's for sure."

"That's not a bad idea," Mark replied. "It just might save his life."

"Man," Herb groaned, "you really are getting to be a party pooper. Or holier than thou. What is it with you? You're always all disapproving. You're starting to sound like my parents." Herb stood and took a swig from a can of Coke, then grimaced and tossed into the trash.

Mark decided not to react to Herb's outburst. It was difficult, but as he thought about it, he wondered if Herb might be more accurate than he knew. Now, why would that be? The truth was he just couldn't dredge up the energy or the desire to party and get crazy with people, even his best friends. What was wrong with him? Maybe it was too much Shakespeare. Maybe he had a brain tumor. He felt like he was spinning out of control, yet he wasn't even moving. Hadn't moved much all summer. Maybe he had that awful disease where the aging process accelerates and you go into senility before your twentieth birthday.

He took a furtive glance in Herb's mirror to make sure his hair wasn't turning gray. Nope, bleach blond; who could tell if it was gray? But he really enjoyed that last buzz that night at Carl's. He could get used to that.

Mark decided to change the subject. "So, you want to get together tonight or what?"

Herb hesitated for a two-count. "Sure. What time?" There was no enthusiasm in his answer or his manner. But Mark figured as long as they could get him there, they could work on him. There was no question about Herb's obvious broadening of his drug usage. He actually looked like death warmed over. His dark hair, usually disheveled at worst, was sticking up in unintentional spikes and looked as if it hadn't seen a comb or shampoo in at least a week. Mark would bet he hadn't slept through the night in over a week; his clothes looked like the ones he'd been wearing all summer.

"Usual time, I guess. Around seven or eight," Mark replied as he stood. "I'll pick up a movie."

It was on his way home that he realized he hadn't gotten around to trying to find out about Deborah and Prince Charming. He'd been so shocked by his friend's appearance that he'd totally forgotten.

***

He could try setting a trap. Nah. That sounded too much like the hapless sheriff in a slapstick comedy, where the sheriff always comes off looking like an idiot. The truth was, Phil hadn't seen or heard anything suspicious since the night nearly two months ago, when Carl and Herb went for their midnight ride. In fact, the three boys hadn't even gotten together since then. What was up with that?

69

Had they had some sort of quarrel? Of course, Carl had been busy working for Joy and Walt Winkler. They had ended up hiring him to work at their marina, and he had been kept pretty busy. Although Phil had heard rumors about Herb, he'd never seen him out and about with any of the usual troublemakers. He had to face it; the three kids were keeping a pretty low profile. That in itself sent Phil's suspicion meter off the scale.

A search of the boathouse the morning after the famous ride had turned up exactly nothing. Not even a stray ash. Phil prided himself on sniffing out suspicious "stuff." But, except for a faint cinnamon-laced cannabis odor there was nothing he could really pin down. Pam had told him to relax, that maybe it had been a one-time experiment. Yeah, and maybe the New York Mets would win their division this season.

Now the boys were getting together tonight. Phil hated spying but, by golly, if that's what it took he would do it.

***

"*Tender Mercies?*" Mark didn't notice who had said it, but both his friends were regarding him with slack-jawed expressions that made them look like cartoon guppies.

"Hey, it's a good movie. It won a bunch of Oscars," Mark pointed out in its defense. Actually, he had no idea what had led him to pick out this movie. It was just sitting there, right across the aisle from the blood, guts and gore section in the video store. Looking at the cover, Mark had suddenly felt in the mood for something a little less violent, a little less flashy. Sure, there was a particularly sad scene where the daughter of the hero, Mac Sledge, played by Robert Duvall,

70

and his alcoholic ex-wife, is killed in a car wreck. But the gentleness, the hope, and the renewal overcame the sadness.

Carl rolled his eyes. "Oh, yeah. A bunch of Oscars. For what? Sappiness?"

Herb joined in the criticism. "Man, if it had to be Duvall, couldn't you have gotten *Apocalypse Now*? It's older than dirt, but at least it's interesting."

"Guys, have you seen it?" Mark asked, knowing for sure Herb hadn't and probably Carl hadn't either.

"Yeah, I saw it," said Carl. "A couple of years ago our church showed it. Now, what does that tell you? A *church* showed it!"

"Well, what's wrong with that?" Mark growled. "What about you, Turner? Have you seen it?"

"Nah, but I knew I wouldn't like it when I heard my mom telling her friends how *wonderful* it was." Herb did an eyelash flutter and one-hand face fanning on the word "wonderful."

"That's what I thought. Prejudice. You guys are so freakin' shallow." Mark hit the "eject" button and grabbed the video out of the machine. "Tell you what. Next time *you* pick the movie. I always end up getting it, and paying for it, and never getting reimbursed." He grabbed his backpack and stuffed the video in, then shouldered the pack. "Have fun, guys. I gotta run." He turned and walked away, past his astonished friends, past Pam and Phil, who were closing up the house for the night, and past Carl's sister, Kate, who was coming down the stairs looking like the Queen of the May. He reached the front door and hesitated as the doorbell rang. Kate reached around him and opened it, sparing Mark the embarrassment of answering someone else's door.

71

"Hey, Gary," said Mark as he walked past Kate's boyfriend and into the fading evening light. He jumped into his car and headed out of town to the interstate, careful not to speed or do anything stupid. He drove west toward Kansas City, trying to sort out what had just happened—what he had just *caused* to happen. He had alienated his best friends, behaved like a spoiled brat, and walked out of the Turner home without so much as a good-bye or an explanation to anyone.

Carl and Herb looked at each other. Pam and Phil looked at the boys. Kate and Gary slipped out the front door.

"What just happened?" Pam inquired as carefully as she could. "You boys having problems?"

Carl said the first thing that came to him. "Mark's been really busy with school and work and stuff. He's got a final coming up. He's probably stressed."

"Okay," Phil said slowly. "You think that's it? You two were pretty hard on him."

Herb piped up, "Well, uh, I guess we were just surprised. We've been watching blood and guts stuff all summer. Or the last few times we got together. I guess we just weren't expecting this," he finished lamely as he gestured toward the video player with his chin.

Phil nodded. "Well, next time you see him you should probably apologize. I'll call his dad and make sure Mark gets home all right."

He and Pam finished locking up the house and headed upstairs.

"So, whatya think?" Herb asked Carl, as they started gathering snacks to take down to the boathouse.

72

"I don't know," replied Carl, now at a loss as to how to approach Herb, on his own, about his concern with his friend's increased drug use. Did he now have two friends who were going off the deep end? Carl decided it would be better to keep quiet about all of it until he could get the two together. But Mark had sure acted strange tonight.

***

Grayish purple clouds were piling up ahead and an occasional flash of lightning stabbed through them. Mark continued driving until the first splatters of rain began pelting the windshield. Then he pulled off the interstate and parked in front of a truck stop. Turning off the motor he leaned his head back and closed his eyes. Rain beat a tattoo on the roof as his thoughts careened in hundreds of directions, colliding and splitting into thousands of questions.

God is in this with us, I know it.

Well, let's see, how long had it been since Mark had prayed? Not counting his taking the Lord's name in vain, which he did on a fairly regular basis. He thought he knew the answer, and he felt a rush of shame as he remembered the last prayer he had participated in. It was at his baptism, and it hadn't even been a real prayer. Just something about accepting Jesus Christ as his personal savior, and he hadn't had the faintest idea what those words meant.

He'd ask Hilda. He glanced at the clock on the dashboard. Eight-twenty. Early enough to catch her still up. Mark dashed through the rain and grabbed a large Coke from the self-serve machine. Returning to his car, he nearly dropped the drink as a man materialized out of the rain.

"I am sorry to bother you, but could you give me a ride?" he asked in a quiet but commanding voice with a very slight accent Mark couldn't quite identify.

Mark's heart slowed to a slow gallop instead of a flat-out, thundering freight train. He drew as much air into his lungs as they would allow and stared at the man. He was neatly but unremarkably dressed in a pair of lightweight gray pants, dark blue shirt and gray tie with an abstract design in the same shade as the shirt. He was carrying a dark blue sports coat. About the same height as Mark, he was probably in his late fifties, with black hair, which was pulled straight back from his face. He was clean shaven.

A terrorist!

Mark swallowed, grabbed hold of a few of his wits, and asked, "Where are you going? I'm heading back toward Columbia." *Please, God, let him be on his way to Kansas City.*

"Fine. If I could ride with you as far as you are going I would be most grateful," the man replied, holding Mark's gaze steadily with his own.

Great. The first real prayer since his baptism and the answer was no. Everything he'd been taught about hitchhikers and talking to strangers washed over him as he heard himself say, "Okay. I'll unlock the door. Do you, uh, have any luggage or anything?" *Such as a bomb?*

"No. No . . . baggage," answered the man.

Placing his drink on top of the car, Mark opened the door and got in, sliding across the bench seat to unlock the passenger door. The man opened his door and slid into the seat beside Mark.

"Thank you so much. I appreciate this," he said as he buckled his seatbelt.

"No problem," mumbled Mark as he pulled out of the parking lot and headed for the on ramp going back toward Hemlock. He watched in the rearview mirror as his drink flew off the roof and splashed on the hood of the car behind him. Way to go.

His passenger didn't appear to notice. He simply looked straight ahead. Mark watched him covertly, trying to stay cool and not be too obviously curious. What was a well-dressed, obviously intelligent and educated man doing in the middle of nowhere, on a rainy night with no transportation, no luggage— baggage!—and no apparent destination? Furthermore, why did Mark pick him up?

"So . . . how far are you going?" he ventured.

"I'll go as far as you go," was the reply as the man turned his extraordinary dark eyes on him.

"I'm only going to Hemlock. It's about eight miles from here," Mark told him. "But I can drop you at the convenience store near the exit." Eight miles was beginning to seem like eighty miles.

"That will be fine. Thank you," said the man again.

Mark drove just under the speed limit, thankful for the little traffic and new wiper blades. The rain was unrelenting, making conversation difficult, which was just as well; Mark couldn't think of one thing to say to this man.

"You are uncomfortable with me, and I apologize."

Mark nearly drove off the road. He'd been counting mile markers and had just determined there were only two more until he could drop off his passen-

75

ger. Not that he was apprehensive anymore. He just felt somehow inadequate. That he didn't quite measure up. To what? More important, *so* what? He was giving a guy a lift, for goodness sake. This was not Miss Manners 101.

"Uh, no, no. I-I'm just wondering if you'll get a ride in Hemlock," Mark lied. "It's getting late and it's raining." That part was the truth. Actually, Mark was a little concerned about this man. Why did such a put together-appearing guy have no transportation at a truck stop?

"That is not important," the man said. "I have a message for you. Listen to Hilda. She speaks the truth. She will not lead you astray. Read, study, listen, and learn. Our Lord and Savior is indeed alive and well. And He died for you. Believe the truths that you have before you, Mark."

Mark was maneuvering the car off the interstate and on to the frontage road leading to the convenience store. He was gripping the wheel so tightly he could barely turn it into the parking lot. His heart was pounding so hard he could hear it over the rain and the sound of the semi pulling out right beside him. He had to think of something to say! What? What could he say to that?

Mark pulled into an empty space beside the store and turned to speak. His mouth fell open and he stared. The man was gone. His seatbelt was still fastened, but he was gone. Mark leapt out of the car and ran back the way he'd come in. Good grief, could the man have jumped out and Mark not noticed? Was he hurt? Mark narrowly avoided getting hit by a pickup, which was turning in to one of the pumps. The driver sounded his horn and Mark skidded out of the way.

"Idiot!" the driver yelled.

Mark ran up to his window. "Have you seen a man, about fifty or sixty, my height, black hair, wearing a tie, carrying a jacket?"

The pickup driver climbed out of his truck. "Man, I nearly killed you! No, I haven't seen nobody except you. Look around. There's no one here." He turned his back and slid his credit card into the slot on the gas pump.

Mark stood in the rain and looked at the empty parking lot. Then he ran into the store. "Wanda, did a man just come in here?" he asked the startled clerk behind the register.

She looked up from the magazine she was leafing through. "Hi, Mark. No. I didn't see anyone. Hey George, anyone in the men's room?" she called to a tall, skinny teenager who was sweeping up Doritos.

George stopped sweeping and knocked on the door to the restroom. No answer. He pushed it open and looked inside. Shook his head.

Mark dashed back out the door and ran for his car. He'd left his door open and his seat was wet. He ignored it, jammed it in drive, and took off past the pickup man, who stared after him as he sped out of the parking lot and onto the frontage road.

How could he have just disappeared? How did he slide out, leaving his seatbelt still fastened? Mark drove about a mile down the road, turned around and drove in the opposite direction for a couple of miles. Finally he headed into town, still keeping an eye out for a tall, thin man carrying a jacket. A tall, thin, *wet* man.

Chapter Seven

She was still up. The lights were on, and Mark could see Hilda's head bobbing around through the kitchen window. She was probably baking and freezing for the Centennial Bake Sale. The woman did more baking in a week than most did in a lifetime.

Mark pulled up in front of the cabin and sat for a minute with the engine running. Maybe he should just go home. Maybe he was just crazy and he should check himself into a psych unit. Ohmygosh, maybe he was one of those rare people who get brain damaged from the scantest amount of cannabis. Flashbacks, antisocial behavior, memory loss. He'd end up drooling, in a diaper at age twenty.

Listen to Hilda.

How did the man know Hilda? How did he know Mark by name? Mark would have sworn he had never seen the man before. Maybe he was one of those people who went to church at Hilda's. But why did he disappear? Okay, *how* did he disappear?

Mark shook off the fear that was threatening to overwhelm him. He had vowed not to talk to anybody about his weird experiences, but he needed to talk to someone and that someone was Hilda. Turning off the engine and killing the lights, he slowly climbed out of the car and walked up the flower-lined the path to the cabin.

"Come in, Mark," called Hilda through the screen door.

He didn't even bother wondering how she knew. In fact, he was seriously considering never wondering about anything ever again. In the past two hours he had been incredibly rude to his best friends and one of his best friend's parents.

Then he had given a ride to a total stranger. The stranger, who had known his name, as well as Hilda's, had then disappeared into thin air, and Mark had nearly gotten himself killed trying to find him. Common, everyday stuff.

Mark pushed open the screen door and was greeted by the aroma of chili. Which was a good thing, because the kitchen looked like the scene of a recent massacre. Tomato sauce decorated most of the surfaces of the cabinets over the stove, part of the ceiling, the nearby freezer bowls, and Hilda's jeans and Miami Dolphins tee-shirt.

"It boiled too soon," Hilda said by way of explanation. She handed him a rag. "You can mop up while I fill the freezer bowls."

Together, with the help of a stepstool and a large amount of Formula 409, they got the kitchen put back together and the chili in the freezer. At no time did Hilda ask what Mark was doing here on a Friday night. She put the last of the dishes in the dishwasher and turned it on. "Why don't you pour us some lemon-ade while I go change my clothes. I look like I've been stabbed in several places," Hilda remarked as she looked down at the pattern on her shirt.

Mark poured two glasses of lemonade over ice and found the coasters. He was beginning to feel more at home here than at home. Hilda found him sitting at the table staring into his glass when she returned, wearing a pair of cutoff jeans and a huge paint-stained tee-shirt that must have belonged to Malcolm.

She sat down opposite him. "How is school going?" she asked quietly.

Mark looked up as if he'd forgotten where he was. Then he gave a quick shake of his head, as if someone had just clobbered him with a stick. "Oh, fine. Almost over. Um, just a little bit more of 'King Lear' and then 'As You Like It'.

79

We'll be finished by the end of next week, almost in time for the centennial." He took a swallow of lemonade, feeling slightly out of breath.

"Ah, yes, 'King Lear'. Now there was a dysfunctional family," Hilda remarked. "It's good you're finishing with 'As You Like It.' Lighthearted, funny, not something you have to get emotionally involved in."

"You took Shakespeare in High School?" Mark asked her.

"College," replied Hilda. "We even did a presentation of 'The Tempest'. What fun. I got to play Caliban.

Mark gave a hoot of laughter. "You? That must have been a riot!"

"It was. I had leaves and fake seaweed glued all over me. It was so realistic nobody wanted to come near me," Hilda recalled. "It was sort of a reverse casting for Shakespeare. Back in his day men always played the women."

They sat in silence for a moment. Then Mark cleared his throat. "Um, can I ask you something?" he started.

Hilda looked directly at him. "Of course."

Mark wet his lips. Then he wet them again. Cleared his throat. This was harder than he'd thought. Where did he even start? What question could he ask that would set the whole thing off, and would require nothing else from him? What a cop-out. If he wanted any of this to make sense he was going to have to do a little work.

"I haven't been to church much. I mean, we go sometimes. I've been to Sunday school and I've memorized a few Bible verses. I believe in God, and I've been baptized. See, I just figure God is always there, and He watches over us." The dam had broken; he couldn't stop talking, heaven help him. Hilda was going to call the men in the white coats with the butterfly nets. He took a breath. "Then, at the beginning of the summer, I had this freaky experience. I started hearing voices, but nobody was there. But I didn't really *hear* them."

Mark took another breath. "It happened at my house. Mom and Dad had gone to a movie and I was babysitting Rachael." He told her everything about that night, including sitting in his sister's room on the floor, including the feeling of peace that had come over him, even including the baseball bat. Hilda didn't laugh, didn't run for the phone, didn't interrupt. She didn't even look shocked. She just sat quietly and listened until Mark stopped talking.

Rain continued beating on the roof punctuated by the occasional flash of lightning and rumble of thunder, much like the weather on the night of his first vision. "Do you remember the date or the day of the week"? Hilda asked. "Was it that first real thunderstorm of the season?"

"Yeah. It was the Saturday night I cut your lawn right after you moved to the cabin," Mark remembered. "It was just before summer school started and I was trying to get a head start on *The Tempest*. I remember thinking it was kind of cool because there was a real storm."

"Okay," Hilda replied in as calm a voice as she could muster. "I believe you, and I don't think it was your imagination playing tricks."

"What do you mean?" Mark asked, feeling a little sick and trying not to sound rude. "You think there was some dude who snuck in while I was downstairs getting a drink?"

"Well, not exactly a dude," replied Hilda. "I believe the Holy Spirit is convicting you."

81

"What!" Mark shot to his feet, no longer caring whether he was rude or not; politeness was way overrated. "Now you're telling me that stuff from the Bible just pops out and scares the—living daylights out of you, like Freddy Krueger in *Nightmare on Elm Street*? If that's what it is, I'm not sure I'm interested."

Hilda sat and watched him as he walked across the room, an act that required all of four steps due to the size of the cabin and the length of Mark's legs. Once he decided pacing was not going to be productive he came back and sat down, picking up his empty glass and staring at the ice in the bottom.

"Mark, I'm sixty-nine years old," Hilda said quietly. "I stopped enjoying horror movies with *House of Wax,* starring Vincent Price. You don't even want to know how long ago that was."

Mark looked up from his glass, an apology ready, but Hilda held up her hand, continuing, "I'm going to give you a reading assignment. You don't have to do it until after you're through with school."

"You have your little New testament I gave you, don't you?" she asked, peering at him over her half-glasses.

Mark nodded and Hilda grabbed a paper napkin from its holder and a pen from the chipped cup in the middle of the table. Referring to several marked pages in her Bible she jotted down some passages on the napkin. "Read John 3:16, Romans 3:23, 6:23, 5:8, and 10:9 and 13. It's really not a lot, but it will give you an idea of how simple it is and what happens when you come the Cross. Do you pray?

"Huh?" That last question caught Mark way off guard.

"Do you pray?" Hilda repeated.

Mark felt heat creep into his face as he remembered. *Please, God, let him be on his way to Kansas City.* "Well, sometimes. Sort of to myself. I mean, quietly, um, not out loud." Could he sound any more pathetically idiotic?

"Mark, I'm not going to ask you to do something you're uncomfortable with," Hilda reassured him. "Many people are self-conscious about praying." She made a sound that might have been a chuckle. "This may sound like the height of blasphemy, but I've told Malcolm for years that the reason Catholics have all those ready-made prayers is that they can't seem to make up any of their own. I think God must be bored silly listening to the repetition day in and day out."

Mark gave a bark of laughter and then quickly smothered it with a cough. Grabbing his glass he started to take a drink before realizing it was empty. Hilda handed him her glass. "Go get us some more so you'll have something to do with your hands. Then tell me if anyone knows where you are."

Mark fled to the kitchen. "I was at Carl's. We, um, had a disagreement," he explained as he filled the glasses and added ice cubes. He carried the drinks back to the table. "Mom and Dad think I'm there," He sighed before adding, "Mr. and Mrs. Hillman don't know where I am.

"There's more," he continued as he sat down and picked up his drink. "I left Carl's house and drove toward Kansas City for a while. Something really weird happened. I mean, weirder than the thing at the house."

Mark looked at Hilda, struggling to keep the tremor from his voice. "Please tell me I'm not going crazy, because I seriously think I am."

"Go on," replied Hilda.

So Mark told her about the tall stranger, beginning with *Tender Mercies* and finishing with his sitting in front of the cabin. He left out nothing; even included the mini prayer he'd prayed when the stranger asked him for a ride. He included his maniacal run through the rain and almost getting hit by that pickup. He even included the seatbelt still fastened. As he relived the entire episode he felt another sense of calm, as if his mental health was completely intact.

Bad sign. People who went around saying they were completely sane were usually ready for the loony bin. Like the guy who is convinced he's a lima bean and is okay with that. Mark took a deep breath and finished. "You know, the thing that really bothers me about all this is it feels—I don't know—somehow--right. Like all the dots are starting to connect."

"They are, Mark," replied Hilda, reaching over and putting her hand on his arm. "There's a trite, overused, slightly overly simplistic platitude that says it all: 'Let go and let God.' Perhaps the time has come for you to try it. I'll tell you a little story. I remember vividly when I was nineteen, attending one of those old fashioned tent revivals. I'd always though I was a good person. I went to church, I read the Bible sometimes. I prayed when I remembered to. Then, as I sat there one night, I heard the preacher tell us that all that wasn't anything unless I belonged to Jesus. I had always believed we'd all get to Heaven one way or another.

"Then the preacher said that all the good works I could ever do were as filthy rags before an almighty God. You see, God is all good, He's all knowing, He's all loving. So loving that he sent His Son down here to die for the likes of me. But the good news is He rose again and so can we."

Hilda's voice thickened slightly. "I sat there in that folding chair and looked at my life thus far: nineteen years of it. It wasn't good. I realized that the

84

goodness of God can't tolerate even the smallest of sins. I also realized that I didn't want to be lost and that all I had to do was accept Jesus Christ and ask him to be my Lord and personal Saviour. That night I crept down the aisle and gave my heart and my life to Jesus. My sins were forgiven and I became a new creation."

"Wow." Aw, man, why did he always come off sounding like a jerk?

Hilda ignored him, saying, "Call your parents and let them know where you are. Then call the Hillmans. It's early enough so that you won't wake anyone. If you wish, you can stay here, or not. Whatever you feel you need to do."

Mark looked up from the spot on the table at which he'd been staring. "All right," he said slowly. "If you don't mind, I think I'll just sit here for a while."

"I don't mind. You're welcome to stay as long as you want" Hilda reached behind her and pulled another book from the bookcase. She handed it to him and Mark read the title: *Evidence That Demands a Verdict* by Josh McDowell.

"Don't get nervous," she said reassuringly. "This isn't exactly a read-cover-to-cover book. But, when you get a chance, read this young man's testimony. It's in the back. And be sure and make those phone calls now. I'd be willing to bet Pam Hillman has called your mother by now. If you come up missing there are going to be some worried people looking for you. Including the police." She handed him the cordless phone and disappeared into the kitchen.

Mark dialed his home to the sound of Hilda's rendition of some song that sounded like *"There is Nothing Like a Dame."*

His father picked up the phone before the first ring had stopped. "Hello?"

"Hi, Dad—"

"Mark! Where are you? Are you all right?"

"Yes. I'm at the Barbours. I stopped in to see Hilda."

Silence. Then, "Are you sure you're okay? Carl's dad called about an hour ago and said you and Carl and Herb had some sort of . . . disagreement?"

Mark took a deep breath and replied, "Yeah, just a difference of opinion over a stupid movie. No big deal. I went for a ride to cool off."

"You *drove* when you were angry? In the rain?"

"Well, yeah, I guess I did," Mark answered, then amended it with, "I didn't go very far, and I came right back." He didn't add that he and a *hitchhiker* came right back. Might as well spare Dad his heart attack for now. "I'm not angry. I wasn't really, just impatient, I guess, 'cause I happened to really like the movie and they were being stupid. No big deal. I'll go over and apologize tomorrow. Or maybe tonight. I don't know."

There was another silence and Mark could hear whispering between his parents. He took the phone away from his ear and stared at it. Oh, man, what were they cooking up?

"Mark?" Mom.

"Hi, Mom."

"Mark, honey, are you okay?" Question of the evening.

"Yeah, Mom, I'm fine. I'm just here talking to Hilda. I'll be home later."

"Well, all right. Don't keep Hilda up too late. We'll see you later. Drive carefully. I love you."

"Love you, too. Bye."

Whew. Sooner or later he was going to have to tell his parents what was going on. But first he had to figure it out himself. He called the Hillmans and spoke with Carl's mother, assuring her that he was fine and apologizing for leaving so abruptly. Hilda turned off the kitchen light and came back in.

"Everything all right?" she asked as she drew the curtains over the front windows. Mark was still sitting at the table, staring at his empty glass.

"Yes. I told them I'll be home later," Mark replied.

Hilda looked at him. "My invitation still stands. You're more than welcome to stay here as long as you want. But I don't want you worrying your family."

"They're good. I told them I'm going to stay here for a while." He picked up one of the books and opened it in the middle. Put it down. Picked it up again. "I'll just read for a few minutes."

The surge of joy that shot through Hilda nearly took her breath away. She managed to reply, "Of course. Do you want me to stay with you?"

Mark looked up at her. "No, that's all right. You go to bed. I'll just sit here. I'll lock up when I leave."

Hilda resisted the urge to reach out and touch him. He needed his privacy, his "space," as they called it now. She walked toward the bedroom. "Good night, Mark. Call me if you need me."

"Thanks, Hilda. For everything," Mark called after her, his voice slightly thick.

Hilda grinned as she replied, "You are welcome, Mark. For everything."

Chapter Eight

The sounds of the night had settled around the tiny cabin. Steady rain tapped gently on the shingles overhead, the ancient refrigerator hummed in the kitchen, and above it, the clock on the wall counted off the seconds. The clock told the correct time six months out of the year because the Barbours never bothered to set it to standard time. Right now the time was sixteen after eleven, time to go home.

Mark felt like his eyelids were lined with #50-grit sandpaper, and his mouth tasted like the bottom of a birdcage. He had read the verses Hilda had listed, finished the Gospel of John, Romans Chapter eight and half of Matthew. He was tempted to finish Matthew but knew he couldn't stay awake. He'd probably go to sleep sitting right there at the table and not make it home tonight. Better to drive home while he could still drive. He gathered up the books and left as quietly as he could, carefully locking the front door.

Later, lying in bed in the dark, he reviewed the evening. It hadn't been dull by anyone's standards. Well, maybe the last part, where he'd sat for three hours in Hilda and Malcolm's kitchen and read until his eyeballs felt like they were going to fall out. But he hadn't been bored. Far from it.

He flipped over onto his stomach, genuinely thankful he wasn't camped on the floor of the Hillmans' boathouse. If he was going to toss and turn he'd just as soon it was in a real bed. His, to be specific. Sleep wouldn't come any time soon, he was sure of it. Maybe he'd just read for a while longer. Rolling back over, he turned on his bedside lamp.

***

Two passages kept repeating themselves in his head. The first was the caption on the picture at Hilda's. The second was a passage he'd memorized in Sunday school years ago. He'd marked a place in his Bible with a gum wrapper and had highlighted the passage from the third chapter of Proverbs: *Trust in the Lord with all thine heart; and lean not unto thine own understanding. In all thy ways acknowledge Him and He shall direct thy paths.*

He was asleep with his light on, his Bible open and face-down on his chest, when his alarm went off. Mark hit the button and turned it off, then lay staring at the ceiling. *Behold I stand at the door and knock . . . lean not unto thine own understanding.* No, that wasn't it. But it fit, in a way. Especially in his life. Own understanding. He couldn't even get Deborah to look at him. Not that it was something Mark was inclined to bother God about. But his life in general was—messed up. His biggest pleasure used to be hanging out with his friends and smoking a little weed, maybe lifting a beer or two. Or four. Regaling each other with tall tales of conquests on and off the football field, which made *Crocodile Dundee* look like *Romper Room.*

Lately, though, he didn't enjoy any of that. Smoking illegal drugs didn't do it. Booze didn't do it. Trading lies, watching gory movies and staying up all night didn't do it. It was like something was missing. From him, from his life.

If only he could go back—where? When? To the night of the thunderstorm. The night he was taking care of Rachael. Maybe if he hadn't gone downstairs to get that drink. Maybe if the power hadn't gone off. Yeah, and maybe if a bullfrog had wings he wouldn't wear his legs out jumping.

Something was seriously wrong. Physically, he felt fine. As he had told his mother, never better. But there was this awful, empty feeling somewhere in his chest, sort of how he'd felt when Grandma Yeats died. Only this time he felt like there was something that could be done to fix it. Just what that would be he didn't quite know. But Hilda knew. And, somewhere deep inside, Mark knew.

"Mark, you'll be late for school," Mom called up the stairs. "Remember you have to drop me off at City Hall."

City Hall?

Oh, man, he'd forgotten. The committee was setting up the centennial booths today. Everybody in the world would be there except for the poor slobs in summer school. Even Dad would go as soon as he was through work, and he and Mom would come home together. That way Mom wouldn't have to take her car. Yikes! That meant he had to transfer Rachael's car seat from her car to his and take it out when they got to City Hall. Plus load and unload all her paraphernalia. Plus, he had barely enough gas to get out of the driveway. Which meant he had to buy gas on the way to City Hall instead of after school. Which meant he'd probably be late to school. Which meant he had to get going. Now.

"Coming," he called back as he threw off the sheet and headed for the shower. Life? Messed up, all right.

***

"Hi, Mark," a soft voice spoke at his left shoulder.

Instant dry mouth. "Oh, hi, Deb. How's it going?" Not exactly a snappy greeting, but at least he hadn't drooled or dropped his books. Of course his books were in a knapsack slung over one shoulder, but you never knew.

Deborah fell into step beside him. "Good. I'm getting a little sick of

90

Shakespeare, though. Maybe taking it in the summer wasn't such a good idea. Everything all shoved into a few weeks, you know?"

She gave him a half smile and his heart sped up a few notches. "Yeah, I'm pretty sick of it, too. I'm glad this is the last week. But I dread the final exam. Knowing Curly it'll be a killer." Curly was everybody's pet name for their English teacher, Mr. Thornton, who was bald as a baby bird.

Deborah shook her head, pale brown wavy hair swirling around her face. "I don't know. Eddie took the course two years ago and said it wasn't too bad, as long as you know what each play is about and don't get your characters mixed up. Which, of course, is impossible not to do." Eddie was Deborah's older brother, now in college somewhere on the east coast. "A bunch of us are getting together Thursday night to study. You want to join us? I mean, you're really smart and we'd, um, love to have you."

She swung around in front of him and Mark almost walked into her. She continued, "You've kept pretty much to yourself all summer. Is anything wrong?"

"Nah," answered Mark too quickly. "I-I've been really busy with school and helping my dad. Not much time left over."

That and hearing voices and meeting my own personal ghost and reading another book besides Shakespeare, when I wasn't trying to get you to just look at me once before the last week of school. "But yeah, I can make it. I can use all the help I can get."

Deborah fell into step with him again. "We're meeting at my house around five. Bring something to eat and share with the rest. I'll have dessert and drinks." She shifted her knapsack to her other shoulder. "I can't believe the school board agreed to have summer school right up to the centennial."

Mark laughed. "Yeah, my mom can't either. I'm supposed to be helping her set up the fried chicken joint. The lady who was going to chair the committee had a car accident."

"Oh, yeah, Gladys Reynolds. I hear she's better, but she'll never be able to get around by Friday." Deborah spun around in front of him again. "Can we help later? I mean after school?"

We. As in Mark and Deborah. Nah. He'd heard it wrong.

"Who?" came Mark's intelligent reply.

"Us," Deborah answered. "You and I. I'm free when school lets out. At least until Monday. Then I have to start working at the hospital gift shop. As a volunteer, which really stinks. But I promised my mom I'd do it until they can get someone else."

"That would be great." Actually it was more than great. It was unbelievable. "I've talked Herb and Carl into going that morning, so most of it will probably be done. But she'll need someone at the counter and to do the cooking until my dad and some of the other ladies get there after work."

They were at Mark's car. Mark opened the door and tossed his knapsack onto the front seat. Then a thought struck him.

"Hey, Deb, have you, um, ever read the Bible?"

Well, of course she'd read the Bible. She was a preacher's kid, fer Pete's sake. He felt his face heat up as if he'd stuck it over a barbecue.

Deborah beamed at him. She looked stunningly beautiful at the moment and Mark kept quiet because he knew he would stutter if he tried to say anything.

"Oh, yes. I've read it through a couple of times. But mostly I read passages when I have my devotions. And I'm trying to memorize some of the the the Psalms. You?"

Mark mumbled a couple of generic phrases as he opened the car door. "You want a ride?" he heard himself ask. Oh wow, almost as charming as hapless Herb.

"No thanks. I'm supposed to meet someone . . ." Deborah trailed off as a car pulled up beside them. The same car he'd seen her in the other day.

With a quick wave and a "See ya in class," Deborah walked over to the passenger side and the door opened and she got in, and that was the end of that.

"Way to go, Mr. Smooth," Mark mumbled to himself.

She waved again as the car sped away. Then it hit him and he felt like smacking himself upside the head. Really smart. They wanted his brain. Oh, wow, the class nerd. Deborah didn't care two hoots about him; she just wanted to assure a passing grade.

Loser.

Oh well. Might as well go and be sociable. It would probably be the last chance to be close to Deborah for the rest of his life. Still, she had offered to help out with the fried chicken. And wasn't that romantic.

***

"Bwa wa," said Rachael as she waved good bye to Mommy and Daddy. They were off to one last meeting before the centennial, which would have its unofficial opening Friday afternoon with the arrival of visiting dignitaries from such far-flung places as St. Louis and Washington DC. Whoopee. Mark tucked the baby under his arm and assembled a sandwich with his free hand. Then he poured a glass of milk, balancing the sandwich on the glass, and headed up the stairs to put Rachael to bed. He'd probably feel creepy going up the stairs for the rest of his life. At least it wasn't raining tonight.

"So, rugrat, what's it gonna be, pink nightie or flowered onesy?" Mark asked her in his most serious tone.

"Unny," replied Rachael. No question there.

"I like a decisive woman," Mark said.

No one disturbed his trip up the stairs and Mark got his sister settled without incident. Four more days of Shakespeare. Actually three, if you didn't count the final exam. He'd already read *As You Like It* through once, so he didn't have to feel quite so guilty going directly to *Cliff's Notes* tonight. After an hour he yawned and stretched. Enough.

He picked up his Bible and opened it to Psalms.

Blessed is the man that walketh not in the counsel of the ungodly, nor standeth in the way of sinners, nor sitteth in the seat of the scornful.

But his delight is in the law of the Lord; and in his law doth he meditate day and night.

And he shall be like a tree planted by the rivers of water, that bringeth forth his fruit in his season; his leaf also shall not wither; and whatsoever he doeth shall prosper.

He closed the Bible and put it on the top shelf of his bookcase. If he was to have a prayer of scoring with Deborah he had to get a game plan. And that did not include thumping on a Bible, because that would be so obvious it would fairly shout "Hypocrite!" Wait a minute. Maybe, just maybe the *Complete Works of Shakespeare* would be just the book to win her over. If he studied like crazy for the next couple of days he'd look brilliant. He'd also look like the class dork. But she'd be so grateful when he helped her pass she'd come running to him.

But who was the guy in the car who picked her up today? Mark hadn't recognized the car or the guy driving it. Must have been from out of town. Which didn't bode well; girls were always attracted to out-of-towners with cars. Of course it wasn't much of a car, a '77—or'78—Ford Fairlane. But as far as Mark could see, the doors were all the same color. But Deb wouldn't be shallow enough to have that mean anything to her. Would she?

The phone rang. Mark ran into the hall and answered it on the second ring, hoping it wouldn't wake Rachael.

"Dude! You going Friday night?" Herb.

"Yeah, after *we* finish helping my mom. You remember the fried chicken joint, don't you?"

Silence. Then, "Uh, oh yeah. The chicken, uh, thing. What time was that again?"

Mark grinned to himself. "11 A.M. sharp. Until Deb and I get there." He let that sink in.

It worked. "Deb? As in Deborah? As in cute cheerleader, who just happens to be hanging out with the Mauler?"

Ogosh. Dave Murkowski. Mark now knew why he hadn't recognized him. Because the only times he'd ever seen him had been on a football field. Usually the creep had been on top of him, trying to kill him. A far cry from Mr. Romantic picking up a hot date. What did Deb see in him?

"You there?" asked Herb after a particularly long pause. "Why is Deb gonna be at your mom's chicken place?"

He hadn't heard her wrong. Deb had volunteered to help out Friday. As a friend. Duh. "Uh, she's helping in exchange for my help with Shakespeare. The final exam is Friday."

"Bummer," said Herb.

No kidding. "Yeah, well, that's life," answered Mark philosophically. "At least, that's *my* life."

Herb sighed. "Anyway, we're meeting at The Point after dark." The Point was one of the features that made the aerial view of the lake resemble Beavis in profile. Too spherical to be a real point, it extended about half a mile from west to east, measured about three hundred feet at the neck and six hundred feet at its widest. Over the years folks had dragged picnic tables, tents, broken-down campers and a variety of useless outdoor equipment out there. Eventually it fell to the kids, who utilized it for parties and less sociable activities. No one was sure who owned it. There had been talk of improving it, building on it, making a golf course, and other endeavors. Unfortunately, the neck was underwater much of the spring and early summer, creating an island that was accessible only by boat. An occasional strong swimmer managed it every few years and got his or her picture in the paper. There had also been a couple of drownings, involving alcohol and/or other drugs.

"After dark. Gotcha. Uh, see you then. Do you want me to call Hillman?"

"Nah, I'll do it. Go study. See ya at the chicken joint. Oh, by the way, I saw Marcia Winkler this morning and asked her if she was going Friday. She said, 'I sure am.' Whadya think of that?" Herb sounded slightly breathless.

"I think," Mark replied, "that she's going Friday night. Why, do you guys have a secret code? Is 'I sure am' supposed to mean something?"

"It means she'll actually be there, within reach," Herb replied, his tone dripping with longsuffering. "Maybe I can get her alone and snag a date with her."

Mark suppressed a sigh, rolling his eyes instead. "Yeah, and maybe the Loch Ness monster is going to drop in for a drink. See you Friday. Don't forget the ten bucks."

Mark hung up and returned to his *Cliff's Notes*.

Chapter Nine

"It's all set. We're leaving about the twelfth of August." Richard came into the kitchen just as Mark was finishing breakfast. "I guess you can tell Herb and Carl now, or maybe their parents already have."

"Great," said Mark. He took one more swallow of juice and grabbed a bunch of grapes from the bowl in the center of the table. "I'll be seeing them Friday at the chicken booth."

Shouldering his backpack, he gave Mom a peck on the cheek, tweaked Rachael's nose and headed toward the door. "I'll be late today. I'm doing the Barbours' grass after school 'cause this weekend will be full.

"Is that okay with Hilda?" Mom asked as she stuffed a spoonful of mashed banana into Rachael's face. The baby did her blowhole thing and Mark stepped aside so that the banana mush landed on the glass door.

"Yeah, she suggested it." Mark took the paper towel and Windex from Richard and wiped off the banana. "See ya'll later." He slipped out the sliding door before his sister had a chance to launch another attack.

"He doesn't seem very excited about Yellowstone," Richard observed as they listened to their son's car drive away.

"Honey, he's an adolescent," Maureen reminded her husband. "We're just not going to get the Beaver Cleaver, 'Gee, Mom and Dad!' reaction from him. Ever again. Deal with it. Look for unconditional enthusiasm from Rachael for a few years. That'll end soon enough, too." She lifted the baby from her high chair and handed her to her husband. Richard sighed as Rachael patted his freshly-shaven face with banana-covered hands while Maureen wiped off the tray, seat, back, arms, and the floor.

"One banana. We could paint the entire kitchen with it." He held up the baby and kissed her little bare belly, making her scream with laughter.

"We just did," Maureen pointed out, tossing the paper towels in the trash. "Seriously, though, Mark is excited about Yellowstone. He's just got a lot on his mind right now, including a certain young lady who, I understand, is already involved with someone else." She stood looking at Richard and the baby. "He may get his heart broken, and Yellowstone will be just the thing to distract him until football practice starts. Then he can burn his—excess energy—on the field."

***

Curly was in rarer form than usual. Maybe it was because there were only two more days left and the centennial was just around the corner. After all, he'd been cooped up with twenty-plus less-than-enthusiastic teenagers for the past eight weeks. It couldn't have been any more fun for him than it was for ninety-five percent of them. But if he mentioned the "Christian" theme throughout "As You Like It" one more time Mark was going to come over the table and throttle him. He supposed you could make a case for it being "Christian" in the spirit of 'let's everybody hold hands and sing Kumbaya.' But as far as these people having a relationship with the risen Christ, it would have been laughable if it hadn't been so insipid and meaningless.

And wasn't *that* holier-than-thou and judgmental. Where was this stuff coming from? Curly made another reference to Rosalind's pious nature and Mark unconsciously rolled his eyes and sighed. Glancing across the table at Deborah he noticed she was shifting uncomfortably in her seat. For that matter, so was everyone else. In all fairness to Curly, though, Mark would probably have been less irritable if he'd gotten more than two hours sleep last night.

He'd really meant to go to bed and go to sleep, and he actually did. For about twenty minutes. Then his parents had come home, and even though they were quiet, Mark woke up. He had gotten up and retrieved the book from the top of the bookcase. Maybe something here would put him to sleep. He opened to Proverbs. He had turned off his light at four-twenty, two hours before the alarm went off.

Now he sat numbly in class hoping he wouldn't fall asleep and fall out of his chair. Finally the bell rang and the class seemed to heave a collective sigh of relief. As they were gathering books and notes Mr. Thornton announced, "Don't forget tomorrow is all review, just in case any of you were thinking about being— sick." He made quotation marks with his fingers. Ha ha. And wouldn't tomorrow be fun. Review for three hours in class, study all afternoon; go to Deb's house, study all night. Good thing Mr. Shakespeare was dead; there'd be a lynch mob after him.

***

"I read Josh McDowell's testimony," Mark announced as he and Hilda sat in their usual places, drinking their usual lemonade. He stared at a knot on the pine table and tried to think what to say next.

Hilda didn't answer. She just regarded him quietly as if expecting him to continue. Mark didn't know how to continue.

"It was interesting." He cleared his throat.

A car door slammed outside and Malcolm whistled as he came up the walk. Hilda squeezed Mark's hand and stood. "He's awfully happy for someone who just delivered about a thousand pounds of chili to the refrigerators at the fire hall, City Hall and every church within five miles."

"You mean you made more?" Mark asked, aghast. He had a pretty good idea of the amount she had put into the freezer the last time he was here.

"Well, yes. I had so many cans of pinto beans left from that sale when Jeeter's Market went out of business. They would have expired before Mal and I could have eaten it all. Or else Mal and I would have expired trying to eat it all."

"Hey, kiddo. You, too, Mark," boomed Malcolm as he came in. "I've got to tell you, my dear, that was a lot of chili. If it doesn't sell do you suppose we could use it for fish bait? I don't think I can eat any more and continue living."

He stopped talking and gave Mark a sharp look. Mark was still sitting, trying to absorb what had just taken place. "Hey, lad, you look pale. Are you all right?" Keeping his eyes on Mark's face he said to his wife, "Honey, you haven't been feeding him any of your chili, have you?"

Mark, who was trying to shift from Josh McDowell to Hilda's chili, shook his head as if he'd just received a blow between the eyes with a two-by-four. "No, I'm fine. Just—"

Hilda intercepted. "Mal, leave him alone. He's had a long summer. Mark, do you want to stay and eat with us?"

"Oh, thanks, Hilda, I have to get home and study." He grinned. "One of these nights I need to get a full night's sleep."

Chapter Ten

"I brought Mom's salsa and chips. I, uh, hope it's all right," Mark stammered as he handed the bag to Deborah, feeling like a first-grader at a birthday party.

"Great!" exclaimed Deborah, as if he'd brought the crown jewels. "Someone brought enchiladas and I think Hank brought guacamole. It'll be a Mexican fiesta."

How did someone who always made people feel so good manage to stomach dating Dave the Mauler? Go figure.

Most of the kids, about twenty of them, were sitting on the floor of the family room with books and notes spread out around them, drinking various beverages and talking about everything except Shakespeare.

". . . dropped out of college. He's working somewhere at a resort on the lake."

". . . parents are getting a divorce. I heard it last week at. . . "

". . . can't go. I promised my sister-in-law I'd watch the kids."

"Yo, Stone!" Bobby Morris called from across the room. "Get over here and tell us how to get through this dreadful class. Or tell us how to cheat without getting caught!"

Laughter.

Bobby Morris was brighter than he let on. But he was too busy charming the girls and trying to take over Mark's position as quarterback to keep his grades any higher than necessary. Mark didn't care for him much. In fact, Mark would love to see Bobby Morris get caught cheating on an exam. Hmmm . . .

"Hey, Morris. Got any other bright ideas in that rock you call a head?" Mark gave his rival a kick to move him over and plopped himself down between him and the painfully shy Juanita Baker, who half-turned away as if she didn't have any idea anyone else was in the room.

"Actually, my number one idea right now is to get this week over with," replied Bobby, as he scooted over a couple of inches.

"Yeah, I hear ya," agreed Mark.

"Everything's ready, "Deborah called from the doorway. "But first—" Everyone lunged to their feet like a pack of half-starved dogs. Deborah jumped back to avoid the stampede.

"Hey, hey, hey!" Mark yelled without even thinking. "Hold it!" He signaled a time-out with his hands and shouldered his way to the door. Placing himself between Deborah and the mob he shouted, "Act like humans instead of a den of lions!"

Where had *that* come from?

But the kids slowed down, a few looking embarrassed. A couple of them even apologized sheepishly.

"That's better," said Mark. "Now, all you . . . gentlemen . . . rein it in and wait for the ladies." He glanced at the abundance of food on the kitchen counter, just off the hallway. "From the looks of things I'd say there's plenty to go around. No one will go hungry."

To his shock the guys actually cooperated, standing back and letting the girls file in first. "Wow," said Deborah, still behind Mark with her back against the wall. "Thanks."

"You're welcome," Mark answered as he stepped aside.

Just then Pastor Stringer materialized as if from the wallpaper and everything went dead silent. "Hey, kids, welcome to the Stringer home," he said with a warm smile. "Shall we thank God for this feast and for the hands that prepared it?"

Over fifteen or twenty bowed heads Andy Stringer gave thanks.

All went smoothly. Everyone heaped plates with enough food to feed a family of four for a month. Mark went last, aware that he'd inadvertently placed himself in charge of these barbarians. Suddenly, as he made his way through the sea of books, people, plates and drinks, he felt like the awkward teenager he was. With his luck he'd step on somebody's plate or dump his own plate on someone's head.

Over the chatter, which had started up again as soon as everyone got seated, Mark heard it. "*Well done.*"

Huh?

Nothing.

It sounded like the tall skinny rain guy.

He stood for a moment, willing himself to deny having heard it. A voice. Like those serial killers hear. Like those heard by people in maximum security mental hospitals.

No. I just did something right for a change.

***

By ten o'clock everybody had had as much Shakespeare as they could stomach, as much food as they could tolerate, and more than enough gossip. Deb started cleaning up and the girls jumped up to help her. Mark and the others gathered books, papers and notebooks, and prepared to leave. Mark started toward the kitchen to get a plastic bag for trash when Deb's voice stopped him just before he got to the door. "I've been trying to get his attention all summer but he's had his head in the clouds. I finally got him to talk . . ." Mark couldn't hear the rest.

He stood just out of sight of the girls in the kitchen. Should he go in or should he stay and listen? Well, that was a no-brainer. He stepped into a shadow and leaned against the wall, hoping none of the guys would suddenly feel helpful and head for the kitchen.

". . . thought you were seeing . . ."

"Not really . . . just a friend."

Okay, that did it. Whoever they were talking about didn't deserve to have him standing in the dark listening like a spy. Mark coughed as loudly as he could and stepped into the kitchen.

Instant silence. Deb blushed and looked away and the other five girls suddenly became busy. Just as he'd feared. They'd been talking about him, and Deb had just lied to her friends. If Dave the Mauler was "just a friend" Mark would eat his gym bag. That kiss she gave him wasn't friendship; it was affection. Okay, so it was just on the cheek. But from Mark's vantage point it wasn't just an interchange between friends.

"Do you have a trash bag I can use for the stuff in the other room?" he asked in the coolest voice he could manufacture. There was a frenzy of activity as the girls scattered in different directions, opening cabinet, drawers and closets.

105

Deb reached under the sink and pulled out a roll of plastic bags. "Here you go," she said as she handed them to Mark.

"Mark, wait," Deb said softly as Mark turned back toward the family room.

Startled, Mark turned back. Deb was standing there in the shadow in her light blue tank top, white jeans and bare feet, a good foot shorter than his six-foot, one half inches. "You don't have to leave right away." She blushed again, looking like the poster child for Wholesome America. "I, um, thought maybe we could, like, hang out for a while."

Eleven possible replies careened through Mark's mind. Because he was really, really tired, he picked the first one that slowed enough for him to grab. "Well, Deb, I don't know about you but I have a test tomorrow and I need to get some sleep. It seems to me that Dave might not approve of you and me hanging together."

He started to turn again and Deborah caught his arm. "Mark, it's not like that—"

"Then I guess you'd better explain to him why you're kissing him. It looks like that to me."

"Kissing him?" Deb had the good sense to look puzzled. Then light seemed to dawn. "Oh, it wasn't what you thought."

She looked profoundly unhappy, which pretty much matched Mark's feeling of profound disappointment.

"Hey, Stone, whatcha doin', manufacturing those trash bags?" Bobby called from the doorway of the family room. He looked at the two of them and actually said, "Oh, sorry," when Mark froze him with his ice-blue glare.

Silently Mark handed Bobby the bags. Then he stepped past him and walked into the family room. Picking up his backpack, he called good night to the rest of the guys and left.

Driving home, he wanted to kick himself in the rear. How petty. How juvenile. How stupid. It wasn't like Deb was his possession. He'd spent most of the summer trying to get her to look at him. Now, after making it obvious to the entire world that she was hung up on Dave the Mauler, she suddenly decided she wanted Mark, too. Or maybe instead. What was up with that?

Women.

He pulled up in front of the house and sat for a few minutes thinking. Mom had a favorite little motto she loved tossing around: "How important is it?" Okay, on a scale of one to ten, at this point in time, factoring in his hurt pride and his damaged self esteem, about a twelve.

On the other hand, in the grand scheme of things, or even the smaller scheme of things, say the next hundred years or so, considering the events in his life of the past couple of months, probably a minus three.

In all thy ways acknowledge Him and He shall direct thy path.

Stop it! Mark banged the steering wheel with his fist. Took a deep breath. Stared hard at a flattened bug on the windshield, caught in the glow of the streetlight. Closed his eyes.

"What a mess."

Who said that? Oh. He had said that. A keen observation, Stone, seeing as your love life just went from nonexistent to doomed, you have no hope of sleeping tonight, and somebody wants you to pray. Now.

What the heck. His eyes were already closed. May as well take advantage of that and see what happens.

"God, can you fix this?" came out through gritted teeth.

Nothing. Not even one of his strange voices. Not even a clap of thunder. Silence.

Mark got out of the car leaving his knapsack on the front seat, slammed the door and shambled up the walk to the house. He let himself in as quietly as possible and went to the kitchen for a glass of water. His mother was seated at the table wearing a sleeveless shirt and an old pair of sweats, with a list in front of her and a cup of herbal tea steaming beside it. She looked up and smiled.

"Hi, honey. All ready for the exam tomorrow? Do you want a cup of tea?"

Mark got ice from the refrigerator and answered, "No, and no."

"What's wrong?"

Aw, man, why did moms have to do that, because the universal answer was always "Nothing," which always started a big twenty questions session.

"Just tired," said Mark as he filled his glass.

His mother watched him "Are you sure?"

"Sure I'm tired? Well, yeah. I think I can pretty much judge whether I'm tired or not."

"You know that's not what I meant," Mom replied, the barest hint of hurt in her voice. "I've seen you tired before. This is not tired talking. Did something go wrong tonight?"

Mark drained his glass, feeling the icy liquid slide down his throat and the intense cold shoot into his sinuses.

"No, everything's cool," he replied and snorted at his own pun.

"All right," Mom said, with a world of doubt in her voice. "Get some sleep. I'll see you in the morning."

"'Night, Mom." Mark set the glass carefully in the sink and walked up to his room.

Maureen sat in the kitchen and wondered about the lack of instructions for raising children. It was so easy when they were babies, but when they got to be teenagers, asserting their independence, what did they have even remotely in common? This person she had carried for nine months, nurtured through diapers, teething, crawling, walking, preschool, and grade school had become a six-foot tall stranger.

Then she sat up straighter. Wait a minute. There *are* instructions for raising kids. She reached for her Bible. Hadn't Mona Stringer constantly referred to the wealth of help for bringing up children right here in God's word? How dense can I be? She mumbled to herself as she grabbed her notebook and started leafing through it. Where was that verse? She threw down the notebook and went the concordance in the back of her Bible. And gasped in surprise. In that abbreviated concordance she found over forty references to "child", "Children", and "parent"! There it was! Proverbs 22:6: *"Train up a child in the way he should go; and when he is old, he shall not depart from it."* Mona had mentioned it one day when one of the ladies had been crying over her daughter wanting a tattoo. Maureen had been half-listening because she had the next scripture reading and she still had not learned her way around her Bible.

Maureen was still baffled by a lot of what was going on but she believed in God, always had. But she was beginning to think there was something missing. She'd have to ask Mona when she saw her.

***

Mark sat and stared at the tract Hilda had given him to use as a bookmark. *"For all have sinned and come short of the glory of God."* Somehow, he couldn't liken an argument with a girl with the importance of scripture. The sad thing was they had had a lovers' quarrel and they were barely acquainted. They had skipped over the good part and gone right to the bad.

Nothing was working. His life wasn't going to get better. He'd live, grow old, die and that would be the end of that. Might as well live it up now. Who cared?

Who indeed.

Chapter Eleven

Mark swiped at the mirror with his damp towel and peered closely at his face. No doubt about it. It was a zit. Right there in the middle of his chin, like a bead of raspberry Jell-O. It couldn't be on his forehead where his hair would cover it. Nah, it had to be in plain sight. "Look at me! Just another reminder that Mark Stone's a loser."

He finished toweling himself dry and got dressed. Maybe if he didn't shave this morning it wouldn't be as noticeable. But, when you got right down to it, what difference did it make? He'd probably never again get close enough to anyone for them to see it.

Mom was scurrying around gathering up the hundreds of items Rachael would require today at the babysitter. "Hi, honey, did you get a good night's sleep?" she greeted as she slung the diaper bag over her shoulder and grabbed the baby out of her high chair. She came over and gave him a kiss on his cheek.

"Yeah, actually, I did," replied Mark, wiping the strained pears off his forehead and grabbing Rachael's hand before she could deposit any more.

Mom headed toward the door. "Bacon and eggs are in the oven. Bread is in the toaster. Love you. See you later. Good luck on the exam." The door closed and Mark was left in blessed silence. He poured himself some orange juice and sat down at the table. He had actually slept well last night, except for that weird dream he had just before he work up. The only thing he could remember about it was that he was trying to catch up with Deb, who was always about a block ahead of him. His feet wouldn't move without the greatest effort. But every time he took a step a large book came out of nowhere and hit him in the head. He was very surprised when he woke without a headache.

The eggs were the consistency of Rachael's rubber ducky. Mark made a sandwich out of toast and the bacon and was just finishing when Dad came in.

"Mornin', Slick. All ready for the big exam?" he asked as he poured a cup of coffee.

"Yeah, I guess. I've sure studied hard enough for it," Mark answered, trying to sound civil even though he wanted to be left alone.

Dad opened the oven door and peered inside, then closed it again. "Good move," observed Mark. "Want some toast?"

"Gummy Bear eggs, huh? No, I'll start over." He opened the oven door again and removed the remains of Mom's earlier efforts, dumped them in the sink and turned on the garbage disposal. "Rest in peace," he said solemnly. He got out the eggs and bacon from the fridge. "Got time for some?"

Mark looked at the clock. "Yeah, I guess." Cool, Mark. Like, could you find one more reason to say, "Yeah, I guess"?

And what had made him say that? Granted, it wasn't rampaging enthusiasm, but Dad looked pleased. Maybe they'd enjoy some quality time at breakfast without a slobbering baby hurling food all over. Mark got out the bread and started making more toast.

***

"So, are you going to tell me what's on your mind or is this something you figure you can work out yourself?"

Bingo. Dad always cut to the chase. He had an uncanny ability to leave the ball in his court while letting him know there were other options. Mom tried,

112

but she just couldn't get past the maternal agonizing. Besides, she was a female.

Mark looked at the time again. He had exactly twenty minutes until he had to leave, not a minute longer. He took a mouthful of eggs to give himself some time to think. Should he tell Dad about John's Gospel? Or Romans Chapter 10? Or his hitchhiker? Oh, right. In twenty minutes or less. Nothing to it. Just tell him about the visitations, visions, and above all, Mark's increasing conviction that his life was in Someone else's hands. Even though that pathetic excuse for a prayer last night had obviously fallen on deaf ears.

Or, how about Deborah and the Mauler? And wouldn't that be fun— telling your own dad what a loser his son is.

"Just girl trouble," Mark finally mumbled, feeling like the biggest liar who ever lived. Well, maybe not liar. Sort of a half-liar. Some of it was the truth. It was just that there was so much more to it than that. And then, like Hilda's flash of light, the truth hit him over the head. There was much, much more to it than that. Sure, he was hurt and disappointed that the girl of his dreams, the reason he'd suffered through eight weeks of William Shakespeare and hadn't dated all summer, would turn out to be that shallow. But he'd live through it. This was not a life-changing event. There was something more, and if he could only get a handle on it he would feel better. He was certain of it.

Dad was watching him. How long had he been sitting there like a statue?

"You want to talk about it?"

Mark speared a piece of bacon and scooped up the rest of the egg yolk. "Nah, it'll fix itself. But thanks for asking." He washed the last mouthful down with the rest of the juice, stood and rinsed his dishes.

113

"Well, if you want to talk, you know I'm here," Dad offered.

"Thanks. See you later. I'm going straight over to the chicken joint after the exam. Me and the other guys are staying until the ladies come after work."

As he walked to his car, Mark suddenly realized something he'd completely forgotten. Deb had said she'd help out, too. Fat chance that would happen now. Oh well, there would probably be plenty of help. But, shoot, he'd really been looking forward to this afternoon. He sighed as he slid behind the wheel. Actually, he'd been looking forward to being with who he thought she was. He smiled grimly to himself, realizing fantasy is always so much better than reality.

The grass shifted slightly with the breeze as Mark walked to his car. "Loser," hissed Klork. "He's going to fall flat on his face with that goody Christian girlie. I foresee a lifetime of addiction, just like his pitiful friend Herb."

"I disagree," screeched Muco through a cloud of cosmic smoke. "He's getting too moral for my comfort."

The grass went still again.

***

Mark and the rest of the class stood around outside the room exchanging last-minute bits of information. Mark kept eye out for Deb.

"No, no, Rosalind disguised herself as Ganymede. It was Celia who dressed as a shepherdess."

"Uh uh, Touchstone is from *As You Like It*; Caliban is *The Tempest* dude . . . I think."

Jeez, if they didn't have it now they never would.

Finally Curly showed up with an evil grin and a large sheaf of papers and unlocked the door to the classroom. Still no Deb. Where was she? They all filed in and arranged themselves in their usual spots around the tables.

"Books closed and either in your bags or on the floor. You know the drill," Curly intoned. He glanced up sharply. "Does anyone know the whereabouts of Deborah, or why she's late?"

Mark looked at the time. "She's not late," he challenged, hearing the edge in his voice. "She still has five minutes; the bell hasn't even rung yet."

Curly raised an eyebrow and started to respond. Just then the door opened and Deb came in, slightly out of breath. She looked . . . radiant. Her light brown hair was shinier than usual; her cheeks had a glow that didn't come from drugstore stuff; her grey-green eyes sparkled. Now, why would that be? Oh yeah, Mark wouldn't "hang out" with her last night so she got right on the phone after everyone left and called the Mauler.

Deb hung her purse over her chair, put her knapsack on the floor and sat down opposite him. Their eyes met and she quickly dropped hers. The bacon and eggs he had eaten not twenty minutes ago were threatening to make a return appearance. The silence that had fallen after his comment to Curly became deafening. Mark dropped his knapsack on the floor just to make some noise. Then he took a pen out of his pocket and stared straight ahead, wanting nothing more than to get this exam over with and get out of here.

The bell rang. Everyone shifted slightly in their seats as Curly began handing out the exams.

About halfway through, Mark glanced over at Deb and found her staring at him. He looked away and continued the exam, determined not to get distracted to the point of screwing it up.

***

The street had been blocked for the festivities, so Mark parked in the municipal parking lot and walked past the red, white and blue decorated booths lining the main street of Hemlock. The celebration would last through Monday, and thousands of visitors were expected. A huge parade was scheduled for tomorrow morning, followed by the inevitable speeches by visiting dignitaries up to and including the governor. There were carnival rides set up in the parking lot across from Wal-Mart, and tomorrow night the fire department would have a fireworks display from The Point.

Mark felt slightly giddy as he walked toward his mom's chicken booth. He was actually free. Summer school was officially over, he was pretty sure he had aced the exam, or at least was in the 95 percentile. Party time!

"Hey, it's about time you got here," Carl called from behind the counter as Mark approached the booth. It was still early enough so the crowd wasn't large yet. Carl and Herb, bless them, had apparently shown up right on time. Herb was overseeing the chicken fryer, and the concept of him undertaking such a responsibility was a little scary. Carl was serving, and Mom and Deb were waiting on customers and taking money.

Deb? Deb was here! She was wearing an apron over her t-shirt and shorts, and her hair was caught up in a hairnet. She was also smiling and talking to everyone and ignoring Mark.

"Hey, dude, I'm early. The exam didn't take that long," Mark answered and then realized Deb had to have finished before he did. One of the guys was going to pick up on it so he changed the subject. "Yo, Turner, that grease isn't doing your face any good. Go pour drinks. I'll suffer for a while." Given the mood he was in it was probably best to stay away from people.

For some reason, business started picking up just after three and there was no time for a break or even conversation. Mark had to hand it to his two friends. Neither one complained, even though the temperature behind the counter must have been around a hundred degrees. They could have left; Mark had told them they could go as soon as he got here, but here they still were, working and sweating like the rest of them. They had tied headbands on to keep the sweat from running into the food. And wouldn't the Board of Health praise that! Mark felt like a fried chicken himself, and even All American, high energy Mom looked a little worn.

Deb, on the other hand, could have just stepped out of a cool shower. Her apron remained pristine, her hair under that granny hairnet looked like angel hair, and apparently no one had ever taught her how to sweat. The way she looked shouldn't even have been legal.

Mark glanced across the street once and would have sworn he saw his hitchhiker strolling along eating cotton candy. The incongruity struck him and he burst out laughing, startling not only his coworkers, but a few of the people standing in line at the counter. He quickly recovered and then paled when the man turned toward him and nodded.

Believe the truths that you have before you . . . .

"Mark, are you all right?" asked Mom, frowning slightly.

"Sure. Just hot."

She continued frowning. "Well, here comes your dad. Let him take over for a while." She went back to hustling drinks, taking orders and overseeing her three helpers.

***

At last three ladies and their husbands came and took over for the evening. Dad stayed, but the five of them gratefully gathered outside the booth in the late afternoon sun.

"Whew!" was all Mom could manage. "I'm never eating chicken again."

"That's probably a good idea, Mrs. Stone," agreed Deb. "Mass-produced chickens and other animals live horrible lives under the most inhumane conditions just to feed us. We don't really need meat to survive."

She and Mom wandered off together, still talking about animal abuse. Herb and Carl stared after them.

"What is she, some kind of weird vegetarian?" ventured Herb. "She probably has a peace sign tattooed one of her body parts."

Mark wanted to smack him. Carl intervened. "So, all set for the big doin's tonight?"

Mark had momentarily forgotten. Now he had all he could do to dredge up any enthusiasm at all. But maybe it would take his mind off the disaster his life had become. No, it wouldn't. But if he didn't go, everybody would think he was weird. On the other hand, if he did go it would be the biggest drag of his whole life. Deb would be there with the Mauler, Herb would probably make a complete fool of himself over Marcia, and he and Carl would hang together like a couple of wallflowers. But Carl wouldn't mind, because he just liked to party.

"This is not a trick question," Carl declared, growing tired of Mark's silence. "What's with you? You can't be that hung up on Deb. For one thing, she's a little too good for anybody, and for another, she probably lives on tofu and seaweed. Of course, there's the little matter of her *being taken already*. Or had that slipped your mind?"

"Fer cryin' out loud, Stone, get your head back in the daylight," said Herb, waving a hand in front of Mark's face.

Just like that Mark realized how loyal his two best friends were. A little rough around the edges, crude, loud, and very obnoxious, but they really cared about him and each other. Mark would have cheerfully walked naked through a forest fire before he would tell them. He glanced once more at Deb and Mom, standing in line at the frozen custard joint, still talking. Deborah was showing her a book that looked suspiciously like the one Hilda had given him, that he now carried in his pocket for reasons he couldn't explain. What was up with that? Guys were so much easier to deal with.

He looked back at Herb and Carl, who were regarding him like a couple of consulting specialists. "You're right. Deborah's taken, Herb struck out with Marsha and life goes on. I'll pick you up over there by the tattoo joint at nine o'clock. Don't be late and don't forget to shower. I don't want either of you contaminating my car. And no funny cigarettes anywhere near me when I'm driving."

Chapter Twelve

About midway up the east side of the lake was a small inlet, which meandered around the foot of an 80-foot escarpment. In the spring, it was a clear, peaceful pool, much too cold for swimming. In the summer it pretty much dried up and provided about forty feet of rocky shoreline. Sometimes someone would get the bright idea of trucking in a load of sand, which would be suitable for one season. Then the rains would wash it away, and the next year it would be back to rock again. The kids preferred The Point for their parties, but it had been barricaded for tomorrow night's fireworks. So, after a bit of last minute scrambling, they all gathered at the "beach," which provided the advantage of being farther from town and less apt to get patrolled as often as The Point, which was a little too close for some of their get-togethers. The Barbour cabin was across the lake, and the nearest neighbors on this side of the lake were the Hillmans, but they were a good two miles further north. A lot of forest stood between the inlet and their house.

Someone had started a fire at the edge of the lake and there were a few logs arranged haphazardly around it that served as benches. Some had brought folding chairs or blankets. Coolers lined one side of the clearing and one of Kyle's friends was collecting the cover charge. Actually, it wasn't so much a cover charge as it was a stake in everything you imbibed in. Mark had brought his own drink—7-Up—because he had to stay reasonably clear-headed in order to drive. He hadn't wanted to drive tonight, but the offer had shot out of his mouth before he could stop it. It probably had something to do with the warm, fuzzy feeling that had come over him this afternoon. Tonight Mark had forked over a ten-dollar bill just so he wouldn't appear too much of a dweeb. Maybe he'd take a drag or two off somebody's reefer.

The party hadn't quite gotten underway when they had arrived, but was starting to rev up with the appearance of a few college kids taking the weekend off from their summer jobs in honor of the centennial. Several out-of-towners were also there, no doubt having gotten word about the party when they'd come into town for the weekend. The mix made Mark slightly uneasy, but he shook off the feeling in anticipation of letting himself go after his less-than-wonderful summer.

The question of the night seemed to be who was going skinny dipping. A few of the girls had walked down the shoreline out of sight and could be heard giggling. One of the guys snagged a beer from a cooler and walked after them. The giggles turned to screams, nearly drowning out Bon Jovi, who was belting out *You Give Love a Bad Name* from somebody's boom box.

"Geez," said Herb, "if they don't want to be seen naked, why do they take their clothes off?" He took another hit off the joint being passed around and handed it to Mark, who handed it to Carl. The air was becoming heavy, and since it was a still night, the smoke just hung around. On the up side, if you wanted to look at it that way, it kept the mosquitoes down. Mark got up and moved to the outside of the circle. At least Deb and Mauler weren't here yet. Maybe they'd have the good sense to stay away. It wasn't exactly a couples' party. It was more like an everybody-get-together-and-get-wasted type of thing.

The sound of an outboard motor joined in the general chaos and a light came toward them across the water. The motor cut out and the boat floated to shore right where the girls and the one guy were skinny dipping. More squeals and screams. A moment of silence.

Two shadowy forms came into the firelight, followed by the skinny dippers, now reasonably dressed. "Hey, everybody," one of the girls shouted over the racket, "Quiet for a minute! Deb has an announcement!"

Deb. Of course. Deb and Dave, making the big entrance, Deb holding Dave's hand and sort of pulling him along behind her. What was up with that? Mark stayed where he was, in the darkness away from the fire. He'd found a nice comfortable rock to sit on and a reasonably flat place to set his 7-Up can. He looked over at Herb and Carl, who appeared pretty well trashed and barely interested in the big "announcement."

Deb pulled Mauler closer, looped an arm through his and shouted, "Everybody, I'd like you to meet my brother, Dave Murkowski—Stringer. Dave, meet everybody."

It was pin drop time. Nobody moved, nobody said a word. Even the fire was silent. Gradually people started talking. Mark heard things like, "Hey, dude," from some of the guys, and more screams from the girls, having to do with, "Oh, my gosh!" and, "Awesome!" Dave and Deb were immediately surrounded by the younger members of the group, while the older ones, and the strangers, after a cursory glance, kept on doing whatever they'd been doing.

Mark continued sitting on his rock. After fastening his jaw back in place from where it had fallen on the ground along with his can of soda, he tried reviewing the significance of what had just taken place. Deb. Deb Stringer. The same Deb Stringer he'd been fantasizing about all summer. The same Deb Stringer who asked him to "hang out" with her last night and he'd said no. The same

Deb who kissed Dave *on the cheek* and Mark had read all the Shakespeare sonnets into it.

Mark turned and looked out into the darkness on the lake, feeling his heart pump hopefully and thinking he was the biggest fool in the county. How could he deal with this? "Oh, so sorry I acted like a spoiled brat last night when you were trying to tell me something."

"Do you have another one of those?" said a voice beside him. Deb was standing over him, firelight dancing off her hair and sparkling in her eyes.

Mark jumped to his feet. "Uh, yeah, in my backpack, over here," he said as he started walking across the beach, trying desperately to remember where he'd left it.

Deb caught up with him. "I'm sorry about last night. I know it sounded stupid—"

"No, that's okay. I was the stupid one," Mark replied, suddenly remembering he'd left his stuff with Herb and Carl, who were now engaged in scarfing a huge bag of potato chips and washing it down with beer.

"Hey, Deb," Carl called out, barely coherent around a full mouth, "does that mean Dave'll be going to school here?"

"Hey, Carl. Yeah, he'll be starting with us. He's a senior, too. Cool, huh?"

Mark located his backpack and fished out a can of soda, opened it and handed it to Deb, wanting only to get her away as soon as possible. "It's kind of warm. Sorry."

"No problem. I don't like beer and I don't think there's anything else here. I don't mind if it's warmish," said Deb, and took a gulp. She was so nice she'd probably drink it if it were boiling rather than hurt his feelings. Mark suffered another pang of guilt as he thought about his behavior last night.

"C'mon, I'll introduce you to Dave." She took Mark's hand before he had a chance to wipe the sweat off on his shorts.

"Um, Deb, I've sort of met him. Our team played his team a couple of times last year. They cleaned our plow. Remember? Dave has sacked me more times than I can count. We're pretty well acquainted."

Deb waved her other hand. "I know, but you've never met him as my brother," she pointed out proudly, pulling him along just as she had pulled Dave a few minutes ago. A sisterly gesture. Not what Mark had in mind.

As they made their way through the revelers, Mark caught sight of two more couples wandering out of the woods from the direction of the road. The place was getting seriously crowded. He had a brief flash of something slightly out of kilter, something about to get out of control. Then it was gone and he was only aware of Deb's hand in his.

Dave was talking to two of the skinny dippers, now dressed in their shorts and scanty tops, and looking as if they would gladly eat each other alive over him, if it came to that. Mark tried putting himself in their shoes and failed. He just couldn't see what they saw in him. Dave would fit comfortably into the tall, dark and handsome category, the kind chicks went for.

Deb just walked right up and interrupted. "Dave, meet Mark. Mark, this is Dave," she rattled off, to icy looks from the two girls.

Mark couldn't think of anything clever or snappy, so he settled for, "Hey, Dave."

"Mark helped the Shakespeare class pass the final this morning," chirped Deb, and Mark wanted to bury himself in the mud.

"Hey, Mark. I remember you, don't I?"

The tone was friendly, so Mark gave him a half smile and said, "Yeah. You were pounding me into the ground."

"Oh, yeah. Hey, you throw a killer pass . . . most of the time."

Mark laughed. "You mean the times you're not trying to kill *me*?"

"Yeah, those times," Dave laughed back.

"Hey, guys, don't talk about football, okay?" Deb begged.

Dave gave her an appalled look. "Why not? Isn't that what everybody talks about?"

"Well, yeah," Deb answered. "That's the problem—"

"Traitor!"

The three turned as a unit to find Herb standing nose to nose with his brother Kyle, fists clenched at his sides, swaying slightly. Kyle, looking genuinely surprised, was standing with his arm around Marcia Winkler, making it pretty obvious they were together.

Mark saw it in an instant. Herb had worn himself out all summer trying to get a date with Marcia, and it looked like the whole time she was dating his big brother. Ouch. That had to hurt. Now, in the shape Herb was in, he saw Kyle as a villain, a traitor and a sneak. To top it off, he probably thought Kyle and Marcia had been laughing at him.

For the third time that night, everyone observed a moment of silence. Mark had to act fast. Just what that action would be eluded him at the moment.

125

But it had to be quick because Herb was shouting things like, "My own brother!" and "I'll bet you thought it was pretty funny," interspersed with some words that didn't make sense to anyone but Herb. It was time to do something, even if it was wrong.

Mark whispered to Deb, "Take Marcia somewhere else," and strolled over to Herb, who was now at full volume, poking his finger into his brother's chest. "You're older than me, but you're skinnier." And wasn't that brilliant?

Mark reached out to take Herb's shoulder just as he swung at Kyle, who ducked and then lunged for Herb's midsection. Deb grabbed Marcia's arm and they ran over to where the rest of the girls were gathered.

It was true Kyle was skinnier than Herb, but he was taller, wiry, and very fast. He had his brother laid out on the ground flat on his face in about four seconds. Herb kicked and struggled, continuing to emit a stream of seldom-combined words.

"Hey, little brother! Take it easy!" Kyle shouted, but Herb couldn't, or wouldn't, hear. The alcohol, combined with the pot, and who knew what else, had robbed him of any reason. Mark remembered that TV commercial about the brain on drugs. There was a perfect specimen lying right there in the mud on the ground. Several people had found lamps and flashlights, and had them trained on the unexpected entertainment.

Mark glanced at Carl, who was standing slack-jawed, watching the proceedings with the detachment of the impaired. No help there.

Kyle was still trying to reason with Herb when his brother gave a mighty heave, rolled over, doubled up his fist and slammed it into Kyle's nose. Kyle went down in a shower of blood, and Dave immediately went to his aid. Mark had time to think to himself, this is really going to hurt, as he launched himself at his friend, who was struggling to his feet.

He heard someone yell, "Somebody go for help!" before Herb's elbow connected with his chin, driving most of his teeth into large sections of his inner cheeks. The pain wasn't as bad as he'd expected, but it did cause him to loosen his hold on Herb's legs for a split second, giving Herb time to lunge to his feet and hurl himself through the crowd of girls, who were standing in shock at the edge of the woods. This was *not* just pot and booze; it was something far more serious, and Mark felt a stab of fear at its significance.

Dear God, please help me with this, Mark prayed as he surged to his feet and followed his friend up the back slope of the escarpment.

Chapter Thirteen

Hilda's book skittered off her lap and slid across the floor as she jumped to her feet.

"Something's wrong," she whispered to Malcolm, who was seated at the table, hunched over one of his books with a magnifying glass.

As he looked up, startled, Malcolm saw his wife facing, not him, but the kitchen door. "What is it?" she asked of the space directly in front of her, and every hair on Malcolm's body stood to attention as he watched Hilda appear to listen to an answer, and then nod once.

"There's trouble at the beach," Hilda announced grimly as she snagged the car keys from the hook on the wall, grabbed her jacket and sprinted out the door. Malcolm snatched a flashlight from the end table and hurried after her into the night.

***

Over the years, kids and grownups alike had scaled the cliff, only to be disappointed with the lack of space when they got there. No room for a picnic, unless you wanted to take your life in your hands. It didn't even make a decent high dive, unless you wanted to break every bone in your body on the rocks below. A few intrepid souls had climbed the face itself, until the state outlawed it when the fragile limestone began to crumble.

Now, as Mark followed Herb through the pitch black woods, up the precarious incline toward the rock-strewn top, Mark knew, with a clarity he didn't want to acknowledge, what Herb had in mind.

Over a girl!

What an idiot.

"Turner, you moron, get your butt back here!" Mark yelled.

"Go to hell," responded Herb from further away than Mark wanted him to be.

"No, that's where you're going if you do this. Slow down and let me talk to you." The inside of his mouth felt like raw hamburger and Mark had all he could do to keep from choking. If he managed to keep Herb alive tonight he was going to beat the stuffing out of him first chance he got.

"Hey, dude, no girl is worth it!" Mark sputtered and then spat another mouthful of blood.

No answer. Mark climbed faster, ignoring the branches scraping his arms, legs and face. Why hadn't he grabbed a flashlight? And why hadn't he kept in better shape over the summer?

**

Phil heard the sound of a car horn through the calm that comes just before real sleep. A long, steady, blast, becoming louder and louder as the car careened into the driveway. He bounded out of bed, grabbed his firearm and his sweatpants. The sound of panicked voices reached him as he hit the bottom of the stairs.

"Chief Hillman! Please help!" Female voices.

Someone started pounding on the door. Phil flipped on the hall light and then the outside light, illuminating the entire front yard. Looking out one of the door's side windows he saw Marcia Winkler and Deb Stringer, wearing identical expressions of fear and shock on their faces.

He bit back a curse as he opened the door, and dozens scenarios raced through his cop's mind: car wreck, drowning, rape, fire, many others.

"Chief Hillman," gasped Deb. "Herb's gone crazy at the beach and Mark's gone after him . . . ."

Phil pulled the girls inside. "Okay," he ordered, "Calm down and try to tell me what's going on."

Deb started again, "It's Herb. He got mad because Marcia," she glanced toward the older girl, "was with Kyle and he hit Kyle and he's bleeding and then he hit Mark and then he went up the cliff and Mark went after h-him—"

"Who's bleeding? How bad?"

"Kyle. Herb smashed Kyle's nose and then ran up the h-hill and Mark has gone after him," supplied Marcia, who was only slightly calmer than her companion.

"My brother Dave has had first aid, so he's kind of taking care of him-- Kyle," added Deb, fighting for control.

Brother?

"Phil?" It was Pam, halfway down the stairs, holding Phil's sweatshirt. Phil reached out, took it and pulled it on.

"Drugs and alcohol?"

Both girls nodded. Phil bit back another curse. "Keep the girls here," he told his wife as he ran out the door. He threw himself in his car and grabbed the radio to call the station.

***

130

Mark paused for a few seconds to catch his breath and look for Herb. He couldn't be that far away; the flattest area of the top of the escarpment wasn't any wider that a king-sized bed. The rest was taken up with jagged rocks and scrub pines. Mark stood very still, not wanting to step off the edge, but also hoping to hear a sound from Herb. *Please, Lord, don't let him have jumped yet*, he prayed from his heart and soul.

There! A slight scraping sound. Or was it the wind? No. No wind tonight. Thank God.

"Herb," Mark called softly. "Come on, pal. Let me try to help you."

He took a step toward where he had heard the scraping sound, knowing that this was the direction of the cliff face. *Lord, please help me to see, or at least feel where I am. I can't help Herb if I can't see him.*

Suddenly, the entire area lit up and Mark was able to make out the outline of Herb, sitting on the edge of the cliff. Herb looked around wildly, nearly losing his balance on the rocky precipice. Then he spotted Mark and yelled, "Don't come any closer!"

Mark held his hands out in front of him in a gesture of surrender. "Okay. I've shtopped. I'll shtay right here." He sat down right where he was and Herb appeared to relax slightly. It was then that Mark became aware of the light source. Everyone was gathered at the bottom of the escarpment, shining lights up toward them. They knew enough not to try to intervene, but did what they could to assist Mark in his efforts to talk his friend down. Awesome. Mark felt such gratitude that tears gathered in his eyes.

Not yet, there's still work to do.

Who was that?

***

Back on the beach, Hilda and Malcolm arrived, having driven around the head of the lake and through town at speeds they hadn't seen since they were in their early forties and had just bought their first new car. "What's going on?" asked Hilda of the first person she saw, who happened to be Carl, considerably more clear-headed, but still confused as to what had just transpired before his very eyes. "Mark and Herb are up there," he answered, indicating the top of the cliff.

Hilda looked up, and the scene above told the story. Herb was sitting on the very edge, legs dangling, and Hilda got nauseated just looking. Another figure, obviously Mark, was seated about six feet in back of him, as nearly as she could judge. Not quite close enough to grab Herb. Malcolm switched on his flashlight and joined the others. Hilda began to pray.

***

Phil grabbed his 6-cell Mag-Lite and his bullhorn from the front seat of his car and tore through the woods toward the sounds of the crowd. The sight of twenty-five or thirty lights trained on the top of the escarpment send chills marching down his spine. It looked like something out of a Christmas pageant, and the irony of it made him swallow hard.

He radioed the station and told them to bring searchlights.

"Have they said anything?" Phil asked one of the college kids whom he recognized.

"No, not yet," replied the kid, eyes on the scene at the top of the escarp-

132

ment.

Phil put the bullhorn to his mouth, and shouted, "Mark, can you hear me? It's Chief Hillman."

"I hear you," Mark shouted back. Why did he sound as if he had a sock in his mouth?

"Don't come up here!" yelled Herb.

"I won't, son. Just stay calm and listen to Mark." Phil looked around and asked the crowd, "Is there any one of you who can tell me what happened here?"

Everyone started talking at once, lowering flashlights and leaving the boys at the top of the cliff in darkness.

"Get those lights back up there!" Phil shouted. "Okay, one at a time. Somebody act as spokesman."

Phil spotted Carl, and although the kid looked totally wasted, he was alive and on his feet, and the relief nearly brought Phil to his knees. But his son was definitely not a candidate for spokesman. He'd deal with him later. Probably ground him until he was forty.

"Sir, I think I can tell you what happened," said someone just in back of him. Phil turned to the tall, dark-haired kid.

"What's your name?"

"Dave Stringer."

Stringer?

"Okay, talk," said Phil.

Dave explained seeing Marcia and Kyle arrive, Herb's reaction, and the subsequent fight. "Kyle is okay, I think. He's got ice on his nose. He's over there,"

133

he finished, gesturing to the hunched figure over by the coolers. Another figure was seated beside him holding a plastic bag to the kid's face. Hilda Barbour. What on earth was Hilda doing here? Phil took a closer look at the light bearers, and sure enough, there was Malcolm, flashlight trained on the scene above. This was getting so surreal he actually expected to see Alice and the Mad Hatter.

He walked over to Kyle and Hilda. "Evening, Hilda. How is he?"

"Hello, Phil. He's doing all right." She shifted the bag of ice and peeked underneath. "Bleeding's almost stopped, but I think his nose is broken."

Kyle muttered something that sounded like, "Eef oh eet eesh."

There was very little he could do until backup got here, so Phil tried to start a conversation with Herb. "Herb, why don't you just come on down and we'll talk?"

"No! Nobody talk to me!"

"How about if just Mark talks to you? Will you talk to him?"

Silence.

"Shief Hillman, Herb shesh he'll talk. But only to me," came Mark's sock-in-the-mouth answer.

"All right, son, do what you can. Help is on the way."

Phil started up the back slope at a dead run.

***

From Mark's vantage point he could see the flashing lights of all three police cars, the sheriff's car, the fire rescue truck, and the ambulance coming around the curve in town and heading up the lake road. It looked like something out of a Clint Eastwood movie, but somehow didn't give him the thrill he got when he was seated safely with his friends in a theater. The only thrill now was abject fear that he wouldn't be able to save this particular friend.

"Okay, pal, you shed you'd talk to me. Sho talk to me. Tell me how you feel."

"Shut up."

"Sho, you jush want to shtay up here all night?" Mark asked as he inched a little closer and spat out a third mouthful of blood.

Herb didn't answer.

"Herb, just lishen to me for a minute. Remember back at the beginning of the shummer when you shed you were going to get a date with Marcia by the end of June? Well, to be honesh wishou, you didn't shound that crazy about her, except for the shallenge she preshented."

No answer.

Mark was really frustrated at not being able to put two words together without drooling and spitting blood all over himself. But he forged ahead. He scooted a little closer. "The way I shee it, it wash jush a big macho shing. I shink you knew you didn't have much of a shance. But you had fun trying."

"I had a chance! But my traitor brother snuck around behind my back. He's always doin' that stuff to me." Herb was crying, and he sounded about eight years old.

Mark had a sudden inspiration. "Did Kyle know you were after Marcia?" Silence. "Well, no."

"Sho . . . tell me how he could be a traitor," Mark asked innocently.

This time the silence was longer, as Herb tried to process the conversation through the impaired circuitry in his brain.

"He must have known. Why would he start dating her if he hadn't known?" Herb ventured.

About three feet separated them now. Mark could have reached out and grabbed Herb's arm, but he didn't have enough balance. He'd have to change his position and find his center of gravity.

Then, as if he sensed something, Herb turned and yelled, "Get back! Don't come any closer or I'll jump!"

Mark scooted back about a foot. Panic was beginning to claw at his insides. Herb was so close to the edge that Mark couldn't understand why he hadn't just slid off. One wrong move would send him eighty feet down to the very rocky ground, unless someone down there could catch him without doing serious harm to themselves. *How could he save his friend?*

Suddenly the answer came. He, Mark, couldn't save Herb. But God could.

"Herb, don't jump. You don't want to die. You always shed you wanted to be a doctor. Think of all those lifsh you can shave. I'll tell you what." Mark searched for the words that wouldn't send Herb over the edge—literally. "Let me do thish for you. I don't have any great plansh. I'll go in the Army for a while, come home, probably take over my dad's bishnesh."

As Mark spoke, a familiar feeling of calm came over him. His fear was gone, and he knew beyond all doubt that all this had been taken out of his hands. He knew he could do this, if it came right down to it, because he couldn't bear the thought of his friend dying. And he knew that something greater was waiting for him, should he have to die. Not that he wanted to die. It was just that he no longer felt afraid, as he asked Jesus to come into his heart. He bowed his head and prayed silently, "Jesus, I know I'm no prize. I can't seem to do anything right. But you can. You lived a perfect life and died for the likes of me. Please take over now. I give it all to you. The past, the present and the future."

The look Herb was giving Mark could only be described as incredulous—one of those vocabulary words that most kids misspelled. "*Are you crazy?*"

Good. Herb was distracted. Mark moved closer to the edge, still keeping his distance from Herb. Herb started to reach for Mark and the layer of limestone gave way under the weight shift. Mark lunged forward and they grabbed each others' wrists as Herb went feet first over the side.

Chapter Fourteen

Phil heard the shouts of the people on the beach, and the words, "He's falling, he's falling!" His dead run at the foot of the cliff had been hampered by rocks, shrubbery, and tree roots, which he stumbled over in spite of his high-powered light. Swearing a blue streak, he redoubled his efforts to get to the top, heartened by the sounds of emergency vehicles arriving. He got back on his radio. "We need a net, now!"

Hilda watched in horror as the scene began to unfold in slow motion. Herb was sitting on the edge of the cliff; then he seemed to turn slightly; he appeared to be reaching for something; then he slid off the edge and dangled there. The people with the lights gave a collective gasp, and Hilda dropped to her knees and began to pray again as she had never prayed before.

***

Mark's shoulder was dislocated, he was sure of it. He'd felt the gentle "pop," followed closely by the unspeakable agony that shot down his arm and up his neck, and he willed himself not to faint or throw up. If he did, all was lost. To have come this far and then throw up on his best friend as they fell to their deaths would have been too much.

"Hang on," he ordered Herb between gritted teeth. Herb, who wore a look of shock, panic and bewilderment all at once, said nothing. Mark bit down hard on the inside of his mouth again to take his mind off the agonizing pain in his shoulder.

Herb found his voice. "Don't let me go!" he screamed.

This time Mark shouted as loudly as he could, actually only able to man-

138

age a level just above a whisper. "Herb, hang on to me. I can't hold you; I think my shoulder ish dishlocated." He didn't know if Herb heard him or not, but his friend continued to hang on with a bone-crushing grip.

Two very gleeful demons pranced around just below where the limestone had given way. Muco yelled, "Get up there and see what the Stone kid is hanging onto. We need to get him to let go." Klork slithered up the side of the cliff and located what was keeping the boys from plunging to their deaths. Using every ounce of force he could muster he began pushing against the sorry excuse for a tree Mark was holding.

***

Mark had grabbed the only thing he could when Herb went over the side. It was a small evergreen that stuck up out of a narrow fissure in the limestone. It wasn't much, but it was all Mark had. If it pulled out, they were both dead. He could feel Herb's grip weakening and he heard himself say, "Lord God, I can't hold on. Pleash hold on for me." Then he looked down and there was Hilda on her knees with Malcolm beside her. He thought he saw his hitch hiker but he couldn't be sure; he was too busy trying not to die. Herb's hand slipped a little more. Mark tried to hold on but he couldn't feel his own hand. Another chunk of limestone gave way under his armpit, and then the tiny tree he'd been holding lost its grasp on its fragile foundation. It gently broke away from the limestone and Mark closed his eyes and let go of everything.

***

Klork was about to congratulate himself when he felt Muco's breath on his neck. "Out, out, out of here!" his comrade shrieked as he blew past him. Klork glanced above and saw what had made Muco disappear in a split second. Stellarus! The angel's light was so bright Klork nearly evaporated right there. Which, of course, would mean he would be in outer darkness for the rest of eternity. Which meant there would be no more missions of destruction. The angel stood glaring down at him and, for the first time in his thousands of years, the serpetine demon let out a squeek instead of a hiss. The angel opened his mouth and Klork gathered all of his energy and shot after Muco.

***

A strong hand gripped the waistband of Mark's shorts and another gripped Herb's arm. A voice said, "I've got you. You're fine." Mark felt himself being pulled back from the edge of the cliff. He was aware on some level that Herb had stopped screaming.

Then they were lying side by side on the flat top of the escarpment. Through a haze of pain Mark heard Herb shout, "Over here!" and he looked around to thank their savior. It was too dark to see anyone, but then Chief Hillman was there, and Herb was still alive, and Mark was still alive, and that was all that mattered right then.

Mark tried to sit up, heard Herb say something about a dislocated shoulder. He whispered a prayer of thanks and then finally allowed himself the luxury of fainting.

***

The inside of his mouth felt like road kill. Mark opened his eyes and squinted at the bright light right above him. His mother's worried face hovered there, too. He glanced past her and, sure enough, there was Dad. And there, also,

140

was an EKG machine, an IV pole, and a dressing cart, none of which was involved with him at the moment, thank God. Then he closed his eyes again and enjoyed the absence of pain in his shoulder. It was sore, but the excruciating, throbbing pain was gone. Then he remembered Chief Hillman kneeling beside him, popping it back into place before the paramedics even got there. He also remembered Herb's white face floating around, and bright lights, and Hilda and Malcolm, like a potpourri of stimuli coming at him from everywhere.

He'd wanted to walk back down the slope, but every time he stood he got so dizzy and nauseated that his knees buckled. So they'd loaded him on a stretcher and Herb had walked beside him all the way down, chanting things like, "You saved my life. Thanks, man. I owe you big time. You're a true friend . . ." until Mark finally told him to shut up.

Somewhere along the line they'd given him something for pain and now he was fighting it, wanting to know what happened when the rest of the cops got to the party, how Hilda had gotten there, where Deb was.

"Hi, honey," his mother said now, taking his hand and bringing it to her cheek, a gesture so tender that Mark felt tears gathering, and he blinked them back as she slipped another ice chip into his mouth.

"Hi, Mom. When are they going to let me out of here?"

Actually what he said sounded more like he had a mouthful of mattress stuffing, but his parents seemed to understand him okay. He felt around his mouth with his tongue and encountered a couple of knotted strings that he decided must be stitches.

"As soon as they wrap your shoulder," Dad answered. "Is that pain medication kicking in yet?"

Mark grimaced. "Yeah, but I don't really want to go to shleep. Ish Herb okay? Whersh Hilda? What happened—"

The curtain was pulled aside and a tired-looking doctor came in, followed by a grumpy-looking nurse. The doctor ignored him, speaking directly to Mark's parents. "Our hero's blood test was negative for alcohol, drugs, everything," he reported, looking a little disappointed.

"I could have told you that," Mark muttered to the room at large. His parents looked so relieved it was almost comical.

"Whersh Herb?" Mark asked. "Kyle okay?"

The doctor walked out.

Mom and Dad exchanged glances and the nurse started wrapping his shoulder. After fifty or sixty passes around his chest she stopped and secured the wrapping with ties, tape, and probably super glue. He still didn't know what had happened to Herb.

The nurse, whose name tag said her name was Lisa, read a litany of instructions to Mom and Dad from a sheet of paper, and Mom signed it in about eleven places. Lisa scurried out of the room.

"Ready?" asked Dad as he helped Mark off the table, as if he was in danger of falling or escaping. Mom was holding what was left of his shirt, and she looked at it and then him, shook her head, and tossed it in the trash.

Chief Hillman stuck his head around the curtain. "Y'all leaving? I'll be over tomorrow. Got a couple of questions for Mark."

"Sure," answered Dad.

"Look," said Mark, "I realizhe I'm jusht the kid, but could shomeone pleash tell me where my friend Herb ish? And Kyle?"

Phil looked at him. "Kyle's fine. He'll be carrying around an ice pack for a long time. Herb's upstairs. They're keeping him overnight just to be sure the strange mixture of drugs in his bloodstream doesn't kill him. That's what I want to ask you about."

"Me?" asked Mark.

"Yes, you drove him to the party," Phil answered. "I'll see you tomorrow." He disappeared.

"What did he mean by that?" asked Mark of no one in particular. He backtracked. "And what did the doc mean by 'our hero?'"

Dad draped his sweatshirt around Mark's shoulders as they started out through the maze of cubbyholes, curtains and stainless steel that made up the emergency room "You saved Herb's life," he explained.

"No I didn't," protested Mark. "He held onto *me* until Shief Hillman got there."

Mom and Dad exchanged another one of those meaningful looks.

"Let's get you home," said Mom. "We'll talk there."

"I gotta she Herb," Mark insisted. "Jush for a shecond." He was drooling and he didn't even care.

Dad sighed. Looked at his watch. "Okay. Let me see if I can get you up there without breaking too many of their rules."

He wandered off, and Mom and Mark sat down in the ER waiting room. The pain medication was beginning to make parts of his brain feel like dandelion

143

fluff and he concentrated on staying awake just until he could see Herb. Mom was holding his hand and still clutching the Styrofoam cup with the melting ice chips. Mark took it from her, spooned the rest of the ice into his mouth and poured the remaining water over his head. It helped a little.

Mom took his hand. "Mark, I have something to tell you."

Uh oh. She couldn't be pregnant again. But it was one of those tones of voice that shrieked serious. Mark braced himself.

"Yesterday after we left the chicken booth Deborah and I had a long talk. Her mom and I have talked a lot this summer, too, and I've attended some of her Bible studies."

She took Mark's free hand. "Honey, I have accepted Jesus Christ as my Lord and Savior."

Something broke inside of Mark. With his good arm he gave his mother a half hug, burying his face in her shoulder. "Oh, Ma, me too. I had no idea—I've been sho tied up with everyshing. Hilda kept me from doing the really shtupid shtuff. But I think it wash her praying that kept me from really falling."

He was pretty sure he wasn't making a lot of sense but he didn't care. Mom stroked his back the way he sometimes did Rachael's. Right now he felt approximately Rachael's age. Richard found them in each other's arms, laughing, crying and both talking at once. He hesitated briefly, determined it was not another disaster, and cleared his throat. "We can go up for a few minutes. Normally they don't allow people wandering around the hospital at three in the morning, but they said this is a special case."

***

Herb was awake. Barely. His parents were sitting by the bed wearing identical deer-in-the-headlight expressions. They stood when Mark came in, and on their way out Herb's mother hugged Mark and said, "Thank you." The Turners joined Mark's parents outside the door.

"Hey," said Mark as he approached the bed.

"Yo," Herb responded. He looked somehow smaller than he really was, lying there wearing a hospital gown, with a sheet pulled up to his armpits. Yellow IV fluid dripped from a bag attached to a machine and ran into his left arm. For the first time since Mark had known him his friend looked subdued.

"You all right?" asked Mark, suddenly at a loss for words.

"Yeah, I'm okay, thanks to you."

"Nah, I didn't do anyshing—"

"You pulled me back. Man, that was amazing," insisted Herb, finally getting some animation.

"No," Mark repeated, "that wash Shief Hillman."

Herb narrowed his bloodshot eyes. "I don't think so. Ask him."

"I'll do that. Sho, now what? When do you get out of here?"

Herb looked unhappy. "I'm going into rehab. My folks are sending me to Wisconsin." He brightened slightly. "Maybe it's just as well . . ."

He sobered again. "You were gonna jump for me, weren't you?"

Mark shrugged.

"Why?" Herb asked quietly.

Mark gave him a long look. "You're my friend."

They awkwardly shook hands.

145

"Don't forget to write," said Mark. "Hey, maybe you'll meet shum chick."

"Who knows?" replied Herb.

"Herb, I'll pray for you," Mark said as clearly as he could. He reached into the back pocket of his shorts and brought out a very battered and well-worn little book. "Take this. Read it in your shpare time; you'll probably have lotsh of it. If you don't want to read it all, read the parts I've highlighted."

He picked up Herb's free hand and stuck the book under it. "Don't forget to write."

"Um," said Herb.

***

Back in the tunnel between the Stones' house and the funeral home Muco and Klork huddled against a wall, shivering in fear. Not that they would admit it, even to each other. Muco was sucking on a fag and the sulfuric smoke rose lazily to the ceiling. He spoke. "You realize that Stone kid got saved, don't you? Which means that we failed."

"But the other two aren't," Klork pointed out. "We can still work on them, can't we?" He wished his scales weren't rattling so loudly. But that was a close call, the closest they'd ever experienced, when Stellarius shown up with all that celestial light surrounding him. To the two demons just the light would have been enough to send them slithering away. But when the angel pointed and ordered in a voice that sounded like Niagara Falls amplified a million times, "In the name of Jesus Christ, begone!" it was their undoing.

Now the demons simply hovered in the darkness, thankful to all the evil spirits that had saved them from certain termination. Maybe they'd get another chance. But . . . Stellarius! It must be a really heavy duty revival in the making to have him show up. And now that he *had* shown up the news would go directly to the bottom. Satan would surely hear about it; Satan loathed revivals. They were doomed.

Chapter Fifteen

Warm salt water mouthwash and ice cream had become his new best friends. The swelling had lessened considerably and Mark no longer sounded like a wino when he talked. He sat on the couch in the living room, surrounded by Chief Hillman, his parents, and Rachael, who was busy playing with Mark's bare toes. After the initial shock of moving his extremities earlier today when he woke up, the pain had pretty much subsided into a dull ache. His shoulder was still wrapped and would remain so for a while. The bad news was he wouldn't be starting football practice in three weeks. Apparently the MRI he'd had last night showed that he'd torn a bunch of stuff in his shoulder in addition to dislocating it and it had to heal. If it didn't heal right he might have to have surgery. He could live with that, but the thought of Bobby Morris playing quarterback made his head ache.

"Tell me what you remember about picking up Carl and Herb. Did you pick them up together? Did you notice anything different about either of them?" Chief Hillman, seated in the recliner, gave Mark one of his "cop" looks. Mark knew he'd already grilled Carl about this and just wanted to see if they had the same story.

Mark remembered it clearly. "I picked them up at that tattoo booth next to the pretzel joint outside the barricade. Herb was thinking about getting 'Marcia' tattooed on his . . ." He stopped.

Chief Hillman grimaced. "Okay, that's what Carl told me. But, did Herb seem different? Wired?"

"No, no more than usual for Herb," Mark said slowly. He hesitated.

148

"What kind of drugs did they find?"

"Other than alcohol and cannabis, he had trace amounts of ecstasy and cocaine."

Oh, man, that was serious. For years Mark and his friends had partied, thinking that a beer here and there and some quality pot weren't that bad. Heck, everybody did it. Then Mark had come to realize that, yeah, it *was* bad. But ecstasy? Coke? That was city stuff. For the big guys. How had it found its way to Hemlock?

Over the interstate, stupid.

Phil started talking again. "We made quite a few arrests last night. We've let most of them go because we didn't find anything on any of them." He rubbed one eye with the ball of his thumb. It occurred to Mark that Chief Hillman probably hadn't been to bed yet. It dawned on Mom, too, because she stood and announced she was going to make another pot of coffee.

Phil asked a few more questions but Mark couldn't come up with anything new. After two cups of coffee he stood and said, "I've got some more paperwork to do, and it'll probably take me a year. Thanks, Mark. I'll be in touch. Carl is grounded for the rest of his natural life, so you won't see him until school opens." He glanced at Dad. "Sorry about Yellowstone. It would have been a great vacation."

The three of them walked to the door with Chief Hillman. After their good-byes, Mark followed him out the door. "Thanks for saving us up there. Herb was losing his grip and I couldn't hold on at all."

The chief gave Mark a puzzled look. "You must have done something right, son. When I got there you'd already pulled Herb back up." He left, and Mark watched him walk to his Explorer, climb in and drive away.

Mark walked slowly back to the living room, where his parents were talking quietly and Rachael was asleep on the floor with her head pillowed on one of Mark's tennies. Mark scooped her up with his good arm and settled back on the couch, holding her close. Mom and Dad went to get ready for work at the centennial, and Mark began to review last night for the hundredth time.

It came to him just as Hilda pulled up in front of the house. Mom and Dad had left with Rachael, and Mark had gone upstairs and gotten his Bible. He flipped through until he found the part he'd highlighted the night he couldn't sleep. He had read Romans chapter 10 over and over. But what jumped out at him suddenly made everything fall into place:

The voice that spoke on top of the cliff last night hadn't been that of Chief Hillman. "I've got you. You're safe." No. "You're mine." That was it. The voice had said, "You're *mine*."

Hilda arrived a little later bearing enough applesauce for several potlucks. She found Mark grinning from ear to ear.

Chapter sixteen

It had been less than twenty-four hours and already he felt as if he'd lived on this couch his whole life. Actually, he felt like a king holding court. Herb's mother had called and told him she was stopping by at noon to bring him lunch. Then Deb had called. She was coming this afternoon to tell him about last night— the part he'd missed.

Hilda had spent an hour listening to him tell about his experience last night. Then, while he ate nearly a pint of her applesauce—the closest thing to her pie he could handle—he'd listened to her version.

"Wow, you mean a voice actually told you to come to the beach?" he asked, amazed.

"Well, no, not exactly. I just knew you were in trouble, and I knew where to go because that was the most logical place."

Then she told him about her prayer companion, and how she knew beyond a shadow of a doubt that Mark and Herb would be all right.

"Mark, I saw you pull back from the edge of the cliff," she explained. "I know you're strong, but I also know that it wasn't you who pulled the two of you back."

"No," agreed Mark. "It sure wasn't. I didn't even know if I had an arm left; for all I knew it was gone."

He hesitated, and then said, "I prayed for help. I wasn't very specific, but I knew God was pretty much aware of the situation. And I knew that if I died, I didn't want to die not knowing where I was going. And I knew that, with my track record, only One could take away all that mess. Does that make sense?"

Hilda beamed. "It makes perfect sense."

"Want to hear some of the best news?" It was Mark's turn to beam.

"Can you top that?" asked Hilda.

"Mom got saved yesterday." He waited for that to sink in.

"Hilda's eyes filled with tears of joy. "I believe we're about to have a re-vival," she whispered. "Malcolm asked me some questions last night about how to be sure where you are going when you die."

***

"I brought you a milkshake." Deb carefully set the shake, size huge, on a napkin on the end table. And wouldn't that go well with the ice cream he'd had for breakfast, Hilda's applesauce, and Mrs. Turner's homemade soup. If this kept up, playing football wouldn't be an issue, but a gastric bypass would certainly be a possibility. Mark remembered to thank her.

Deb planted herself in the big recliner and folded her legs under her. She regarded Mark for a moment. "I've never seen a real hero," she finally said.

Mark wanted to moan out loud. Instead he said, "Oh, man, Deb, I'm not a hero."

"Yes, you are," Deb persisted. "But I know it embarrasses you, so I won't say anything more. Marcia and I had to stay at the Hillmans' last night so we didn't see what happened. But we heard. The whole town knows."

The truth was that it embarrassed him only because he knew it wasn't he who had saved Herb. "Tell me about Dave," he asked to cover his confusion.

She twisted a tendril of hair around her finger. "My father's sister—my

152

Aunt Valerie—had a baby when she was twenty. The guy wouldn't marry her. She did the best she could, but she had a drug and drinking problem. My dad took care of her financially, but Dave had, um, emotional problems. She finally ended up sending him to a military school. You know, one of those that don't admit they're really for troubled kids."

"He seems all right now," said Mark, puzzled.

Deb laughed. "Amazing, isn't it? He was one of those rare ones who get better in spite of everything. Then, two years ago, Val got Leukemia. When Dave found out, he insisted on going back home to take care of her. I still didn't know anything about it. I'd had a first cousin for fourteen years and didn't even know it. Oh, I knew I had a distant relative somewhere, but I didn't know I had an aunt and a cousin in St. Louis." She looked very sad, and Mark wanted to take her hand. Unfortunately, her hand was too far to reach with his left hand and his right hand was strapped down. If he tried to reach her he'd tip over, and he really didn't want to make a fool of himself one more time in front of Deb. Handholding could come later.

Deb stood and walked over to the tall bookcase, which held a dozen family photos. She picked up one of the four of them taken the day Mom brought Rachael home from the hospital. "Anyway, when Val went into hospice, Dave started spending time with us. I was so thrilled to have a cousin! Then Val died last year and Dave got put into a foster home."

Deb replaced the photo and sat back down. "Dad worked day and night for a solid year to adopt him. We kept it quiet in case it fell through. It became official the night before the Shakespeare exam." Her smile was radiant. "So now I have another brother!"

Mark smiled back, feeling his heart rate rev up a notch. "That is so cool!" She had no idea how cool it was that Dave was her *brother*. He decided to take the plunge. "Did you know I signed up for the Shakespeare class because you did?"

Deb gave him a very level look. "Yes, I did." She looked down and a pink suffused her cheeks. "That's why I couldn't understand why you practically ignored me all summer."

Mark sat up straighter. "Do you have a few minutes, Deb? Because I want to tell you about my summer. All of it."

Special thanks to my friend and comrade in widowhood, Eileen Bunch, who read the very rough first draft of my book. She relentlessly pursued and apprehended countless errors, typos, comma splices, and those other picky details that drive authors and readers nuts. Thank you, Eileen. I love you. Any errors are not her fault.

Thanks also to my pastor, Bob Clark, who held me accountable when I was tempted to just say, "It's good enugh," when it wasn't. I am so grateful.

Thank you to my heavenly Father, who takes me at my most unlovely and makes something acceptable to Him. Amen.

24090749R00085

Made in the USA
Charleston, SC
12 November 2013